# *Brown Tom's*

## SCHOOLDAYS

# FIRST VOICES, FIRST TEXTS

SERIES EDITOR: WARREN CARIOU

First Voices, First Texts aims to reconnect contemporary readers with some of the most important Aboriginal literature of the past, much of which has been unavailable for decades. This series reveals the richness of these works by providing newly re-edited texts that are presented with particular sensitivity toward Indigenous ethics, traditions, and contemporary realities. The editors strive to indigenize the editing process by involving communities, by respecting traditional protocols, and by providing critical introductions that give readers new insights into the cultural contexts of these unjustly neglected classics.

Enos T. Montour

# Brown Tom's Schooldays

Edited and with an Introduction
by Mary Jane Logan McCallum

UNIVERSITY OF MANITOBA PRESS

Brown Tom's Schooldays
© Enos T. Montour 2024
Introduction © Mary Jane Logan McCallum, Foreword © Elizabeth
Graham, Afterword © Mary I. Anderson and Margaret McKenzie 2024

28  27  26  25  24        1  2  3  4  5

University of Manitoba Press
Winnipeg, Manitoba, Canada
Treaty 1 Territory
uofmpress.ca

*Cataloguing data available from Library and Archives Canada*
First Voices, First Texts, ISSN 2291-9627 ; 7
ISBN 978-177284-086-5 (PAPER)
ISBN 978-177284-088-9 (PDF)
ISBN 978-177284-089-6 (EPUB)
ISBN 978-177284-087-2 (BOUND)

Cover image: Drawing by Audrey Teather published with Montour's story,
"Too Big For Santa Claus," in *Onward*, 2 February 1958.
Cover design by Jonathan Dyck
Interior design by Jess Koroscil

Printed in Canada

The University of Manitoba Press acknowledges the financial
support for its publication program provided by the Government of
Canada through the Canada Book Fund, the Canada Council
for the Arts, the Manitoba Department of Sport, Culture,
and Heritage, the Manitoba Arts Council, and
the Manitoba Book Publishing Tax Credit.

Funded by the Government of Canada | Canada

# Contents

BROWN TOM'S
SCHOOLDAYS

by

Enos T. Montour

Audrey Teather

**FIGURE 1.** Original cover page of *Brown Tom's Schooldays*. Photograph courtesy of Elizabeth Graham.

# On a Personal Note: The Making of *Brown Tom's Schooldays*, 1982–1984

*Elizabeth Graham*

I only knew Dr. Enos T. Montour during the last two years of his life but count myself privileged to have had a glimpse into the life of this interesting, learned, witty man. In 1982 Donald Smith, the University of Calgary historian, put me in touch with Enos Montour. Don had met Enos in 1974 while researching his PhD thesis. They had a mutual appreciation of writing and scholarship and became friends. Don knew that I was doing research into the history of Mount Elgin Residential School in Muncey, Ontario, and that over the previous thirty years Enos had been writing various stories about his days at Mount Elgin. Enos could give me invaluable first-hand material, and he could use my help turning those stories into a book that would become *Brown Tom's Schooldays*. I was excited to talk to Enos Montour and so it began. I received a letter from Enos, and our collaboration got under way:

10 March 1982: Dear Mrs Graham:... Please send me a Paragraph with this Heading — "By Way of Identification"—Who are you? What Schools attended?

College? What have you published? Where did you get my Story of Burning Mt Elgin barns? What life work, teacher, Haus Frau? . . . Why this questionnaire? I just like to know to whom I am talking if you don't mind. . . . I am glad to find someone who is interested in Mt. Elgin (The "Mush Hole" as we boys called it).

Once Enos had accepted me as editor, he laid out his vision for his book, making it clear that his writings and mine, although complementary, should be completely separate:

17 April 1982: Hail Ye Editor, Having looked over your scientific and well researched book on the Native People, I am more than ever convinced that you are well qualified to be the Editor of "The Saga of Little Mo, Ojibway" . . . Our approaches can be complementary. You have the college essay style—the sociological approach to the problem. My approach is more Human Interest. How these schools looked to the wee "inmates"—the homeless urchins—"The toad beneath the harrow." I hope to hear . . . that you are willing to wield the Black Pencil and the Whip Hand. You may be rendering a Service to Posterity. "Qui Sais?"

6 July 1982: What would you think of producing 2 books: 1) A college text book type for students taking a course in Emergent Peoples. It would be a "no-nonsense," scholarly, well-researched book. You have already done the ground work for this in Mt. Elgin story. You have the list of officials & the history of the Methodist missions. It would be very gratifying if such a book were commissioned. 2) The second book would be more my style, a looser,

breezy type showing the Human side of missionary
work. It would show how these schools appeared to the
inmates, the Native urchins sent to them. A Dickens type
of personal history, thinly disguised. There would be
PATHOS, humor and human interest, a readable book.
It would be a FICTIONALIZED version of Book No.1.
These Books (1) by Ph.D. Professor, with patience for
Research, a wholly scholarly writing. Book No 2 would
be scribbled down "right off the top of my head" by a
would-be author with liberal use of noms de plume. It
would be about no one school in particular, yet about all
these boarding schools. (Book No. 2 would be companion
Vol to Bk 1).

My duties, he instructed, included "To apportion my Homework—3
chapters at a time with guidelines." Thereafter I was "Editor": "You
qualify as editor . . . you stimulate the dozy dormouse into action
and wakefulness." Enos was to be known as "Scribe," which he often
qualified as "The awakened scribe" or, as his health faded, "erst-
while, of sorts, the limping scribe, faint but pursuing, the zig-zag
wheelchair scribe."

We first met at the United Church offices in Hamilton, where
Enos gave me his collection of the rough typescripts of Mount Elgin
stories he had written over many years, and we got to work to orga-
nize them into a book.

Enos had definite opinions about how I should edit. I did make
suggestions for consistency and clarification of the content. I retained
his use of the term "Indian," as that was common parlance forty years
ago. Readers may not be comfortable with his characterizations of
individuals from different groups, but that is all his own style and a
literary device. We discussed what title to use from his suggestions:
"Feathered Urchins at Boarding School"; "Adventures of Ojibway

'Little Mo'"; "Brown Tom's Schooldays." My pedantic take at the time was that the use of the term "feathered" might bother Indigenous people who wanted to get away from stereotypes; Ojibway "Little Mo" was misleading, as Enos's family was Delaware (though part of the "Mo"hican confederacy); likewise, Brown Tom would be better if Enos's middle name was Tom. In the end, we settled on *Brown Tom's Schooldays.*

Enos was by then living in Albright Manor, "sometimes called 'Alcatraz' because of Isolation,"[1] a home for retired United Church ministers just outside Beamsville, Ontario. I visited him a few times during our work together and, as he had never lost the school legacy of preoccupation with food, he liked to go to a restaurant after we had discussed the business of the day and indulge in his favourite lunch of liver and onions. He also enjoyed the trips out to restaurants that Albright Manor would sometimes arrange: "24 Nov 1982: Our Diners Club made 2 trips out. I wrestled a Pork chop to the ground. It gets us away from Pizza, Lasagne and (gulp) Quiche!"

He was in his eighties, with health and eyesight failing but strong in spirit and ready to finish his tales from Mount Elgin. He had nearly sold through the first printing of *The Rockhound of New Jerusalem* (1981) and had had great success with *The Feathered U.E.L.'s*, which he published in 1973. That experience gave him a sense of the market for *Brown Tom*:

> 17 April 1982: MARKET—Not to worry. I have a waiting list of readers for this Residential School story. I have only to notify them that my 3rd is on sale and the orders will pour in. METHOD—Might be a Photocopying job from a properly typed script (Vanity Printing) with a limited number being turned out as Market demands. That method would keep the price down below $10.

6 July 1982: There is no doubt about the Demand right now for Books on Indian Residential Schools. Indian Cultural Committees are discussing the pros and cons of these Missionary Institutes for Indian children, especially since a dark "Dungeon" was found in the Mohawk Institute, when the Woodland Indian Centre took over the buildings. It was kept intact for all visitors to see.

Enos Montour told me he did not wish to write a diatribe against the church. However, in these tales we find that his vivid descriptions of the loneliness, petty cruelty, discipline, hunger, sickness, friendships and fun, church, work, and education experienced by a small boy shine a very personal light on all the elements, both negative and positive in his view, that characterized Residential Schools. Enos was not only a minister but also a journalist and historian. His extensive historical and cultural knowledge and his political awareness, which he explores more fully in articles and books such as *The Feathered U.E.L.'s*, are apparent when he questions the purpose of the Residential Schools and raises issues of First Nations rights and religious indoctrination. The chapter on religion reveals that as a United Church minister who grew up on Six Nations territory, Enos was open to various forms of religious expression. His response to anthropologist and historian Paul A.W. Wallace's 1952 inquiry about the Haudenosaunee Longhouse religion shows a keen interest in and respect for the Longhouse People. As Enos wrote to me on 23 June 1982: "Re 'Getting Religion.' That chapter is not personal. It's an amalgam of '4square' C.G.I.T. Ideals (1925) and 'The Way It Was' at Mt. Elgin. It's a bit of wishful thinking re Indian Religious Awakening. My personal Rel experience comes later 1917, darkest Day of War I."

The brilliance of *Brown Tom's Schooldays* lies not only in what Enos teaches us in the stories but in the important lesson that you can educate through humour. By making these tales readable he gets many serious messages across. Also, he, along with the other Survivors I have met who often laughed as they recounted shocking incidents, reminds us that humour and resilience go hand in hand, helping people endure both the experience and the painful memories. Enos once wrote to me, "I said to a friend at Springvale 'The next book I write is going to be a SERIOUS one.' She said 'Grampa, you COULDN'T write a serious book.' The snickers would come then."[2] I appreciated all the humour in his correspondence.

Enos died long before I finished researching and writing "Book No. 1." *The Mush Hole: Life at Two Indian Residential Schools*, a history of Mount Elgin and the Mohawk Institute, took on a very different form over the years from the companion volume he had envisaged in 1982. It became apparent to me as I did the research that any history of Residential Schools is a multi-faceted narrative, rooted in its own time and space, and another predigested version of events would never tell the whole story. It was impossible to reduce the wealth and variety of information to one version of history, and I had to make it clear whose version I was presenting. As a non-Indigenous person with an English boarding-school and academic background, I decided to present the material from three "voices" and divided the book into three parts: Voice-over, Voice of Authority, and Voice of Experience. It broke all the rules of my 1960s anthropological training to insert personal opinions into a study, but in Voice-over I wrote an overview and analysis of the subject and attempted to be clear as to my point of view and where any unconscious biases might come from. In the 1980s, as I read all the original documents I was able to find from the Department of Indian Affairs in the National Archives of Canada and from church and other archives, I realized that each document told us something different about attitudes, prejudices, motivations, daily life, events, politics, finances, and so forth, and the reader could mine and interpret this information if the documents were transcribed

**FIGURE 2.** Enos Montour outside United Church offices in Hamilton, Ontario, 1982. Photograph courtesy of Don Smith.

verbatim. This became the Voice of Authority. In Voice of Experience the former students—or Survivors—I interviewed in the 1990s told their stories in their own words, allowing readers to feel the emotional impact of hearing directly about their unique experiences.

It is especially valuable to have Enos Montour's illuminating stories of Residential School life through the eyes of a child to complement and supplement the documentary material from that era. *Brown Tom's Schooldays* is a snapshot of just five of the nearly 100 years Mount Elgin was in operation, but as he intended, Enos's personal experiences pertain to all the children who attended Residential Schools, enabling readers to gain the best understanding possible of a situation they have not personally endured. Woven into the stories, Enos's broader commentary on the Residential School system provides a frame for the whole picture. Our two approaches met and overlapped, as *The Mush Hole* contains many human interest stories and *Brown Tom's Schooldays* explores serious topics.

Although *Brown Tom's Schooldays* was not widely distributed until after Enos's death, he did see the finished book and was pleased with it and the Preface. That was forty years ago, and thirteen years before I finally published "Book No. 1," *The Mush Hole*; thirteen years before Residential School Survivors started to share their stories and to bring lawsuits against churches and government; thirty years before the publication of evidence and experiences of Residential School Survivors by the Truth and Reconciliation Commission.

Enos told me he wanted to "leave history to the historians." The Preface to the first edition of *Brown Tom's Schooldays* reflects his wishes. In this new edition, however, we gain a much deeper understanding of Enos's work through historian Mary Jane Logan McCallum's exploration of *Brown Tom's Schooldays'* place and significance in history, and her elaborations on many aspects of Enos Montour's writing while preserving the integrity of his vision. More than a century after Enos Montour left Mount Elgin, *Brown Tom's Schooldays* is still timely, significant, and, perhaps most importantly for Enos, "a good read."

# Enos Montour, Brown Tom, and "Ontario Indian" Literature

*Mary Jane Logan McCallum*

Copies of *Brown Tom's Schooldays* emerged into the world on 8.5 x 11-inch paper from a Xerox copier machine at M and T Printing, a copy shop in Waterloo, Ontario, in May 1985. It was only six months after its author, Enos T. Montour, had passed away at his seniors' residence in Beamsville, Ontario, at the age of eighty-five. The book had a brown cardstock cover featuring an image of a boy and a pig leaning on a fence, photocopied from a United Church magazine. Montour's fifteen chapters, each approximately 1,600 words long, trace the life of the main character, an "Ontario Indian boy" named Tom, during his time at Mount Elgin Residential School, near London, Ontario. These chapters and editor Elizabeth Graham's Preface were held together with black plastic spiral binding. One could be forgiven for mistaking *Brown Tom's Schooldays* for an everyday 1980s university assignment, rather than a skilful and extraordinary literary text of the school story genre and a rare chronicle of Methodist (subsequently United Church)³ federal Indian schooling in the early twentieth century.

I first learned of *Brown Tom's Schooldays* in the late 1990s, when it was referenced in a section of Elizabeth Graham's *The Mush Hole:*

*Life at Two Indian Residential Schools* that discussed the ubiquitous experience of hunger at Mount Elgin.[4] *The Mush Hole* was, and remains, an important resource about the history of Mount Elgin and the Mohawk Institute, two of the earliest institutions in the Indian Residential School system legislated by Canada's federal government in the nineteenth century.[5] *The Mush Hole* is the go-to book on Mount Elgin for my family, and it remains a commonly cited book across the country but especially in Ontario for its unique archival and oral history, and its narrative analysis of Mount Elgin and the Mohawk Institute. Though it is now more than twenty-five years old, it remains a widely used resource; I have heard it referred to as the "bible" at the Woodland Cultural Centre, a First Nations archive, library, and museum located within the campus of the Mohawk Institute.

But *Brown Tom's Schooldays* is not so well-known. Chapters of the book were drafted by Montour as early as the 1950s and then edited and typed up by Graham, who finished in 1984 and sent Montour a bound copy. In 1985, and at the request of Montour's daughter, Shirley McKenzie, bound copies of the book were printed for distribution at Montour's memorial service. The only copy I could locate was at the (non-lending) National Library in Ottawa. Historian and archivist Anne Lindsay put me in touch with a researcher who had a digital scan of the book that he shared with me. Even though it was a copy of a copy of a copy of a copy of the original, every grey pixel was like gold to me, because *Brown Tom's Schooldays* is set at Mount Elgin when my great-grandfather and his brother attended the school. Mount Elgin student records covering the early twentieth century are extremely thin, and so it is difficult to know their precise dates of attendance, but it is likely that my relatives and Enos crossed paths at Mount Elgin. I immediately wanted everyone to read it! Indigenous accounts of Mount Elgin and Residential Schools generally in years before living memory are very rare, and *Brown Tom* richly describes times, people, and events. The insights of this generation of First

Nations people are vitally important to understanding how twentieth-century Indigenous intellectual history flourished in a context of violent settler racism and colonialism that appropriated not only land and resources but also time, language, headspace, and opportunity.

*Brown Tom's Schooldays* speaks to many histories, but for me it speaks most to the history of three Thames River First Nations (Munsee-Delaware Nation, Chippewas of the Thames First Nation, and Oneida of the Thames First Nation) and the community of Delaware people at Six Nations of the Grand River. The book also depicts an experience of federal Indian education at a Methodist boarding school in a way that is specific to gender, as well as to time, place, and local First Nations and settler history. *Brown Tom* elucidates the place of colonial religious education and the barriers and opportunities it entailed for First Nations male students at the time. Montour attended Mount Elgin from around 1910 to 1915. Fourteen years after he left Mount Elgin, he became an ordained United Church minister, after earning bachelor's degrees in Arts and Divinity from McGill University.

The lives of First Nations people in the twentieth century have long interested me. I am particularly drawn to the written record of Indigenous life in the 1900s, and I have found meaningful conversation about First Nations archives within the Munsee Delaware Language and History Group. This group seeks to revitalize our highly endangered language, Lunaape, and to ask questions about the social, cultural, and intellectual history of our relatives. I returned to *Brown Tom* (and *The Mush Hole*) while studying child labour at Mount Elgin with the group.[6] I read *Brown Tom* from cover to cover again in 2019 and referred to it often in conversations and presentations about that project. Because it was so difficult to locate, I found it unreasonable to recommend, even while I did often recommend it. I became determined to reprint it.

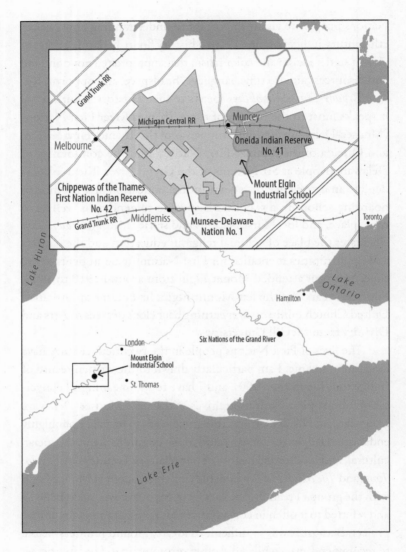

**FIGURE 3.** Map of the Thames River and Grand River communities, also marking Mount Elgin. Map by Julie Witmer. Base data © MapTiler © OpenStreetMap contributors.

I connected with University of Manitoba Press editor Jill McConkey, who thought it would be a good contribution to the First Voices, First Texts series. Jill contacted Elizabeth Graham and searched for descendants of Montour in the hopes that they too would be interested in publishing a new edition. From an inscription by his daughter, Shirley McKenzie, on the inside cover of the digitized copy of the book and information from her obituary, Jill reached Montour's granddaughter Mary I. Anderson, who then contacted her sister, Margaret McKenzie. Serendipitously, they had already discussed a similar idea in the past and enthusiastically supported a reprint; Elizabeth Graham had also been working on producing a new edition of *Brown Tom* but had been unable to track down Enos's granddaughters for permission.

When I first met with Elizabeth, Jill, Margaret, and Mary, it was through online video conferencing in the summer of 2021. During that conversation, we discussed Montour's many allusions to classic literature and the Bible. Montour's writing indeed reflects his education and his literary skill and dedication, his love of literature, history, and parody, and the joy he found in reading and writing. *Brown Tom* makes me think about an encounter I once had with a historian of Western Canada, who suggested in his analysis of Indigenous history education that First Nations people disdained books and book learning, preferring oral and practical education. I knew his conclusion was narrow-minded and unrealistic then, and it still annoys me today. But my own ability to read Montour is limited because of my late twentieth- and early twenty-first-century primary and secondary education in Canada and my training as a historian (rather than a literary scholar), and I needed reference points to come to a better understanding of the book. Some readers may not face these issues, but for those like me, I have included tables of Montour's literary and biblical allusions, including references noted by Elizabeth Graham in her original Preface to the book, in Appendix 1.

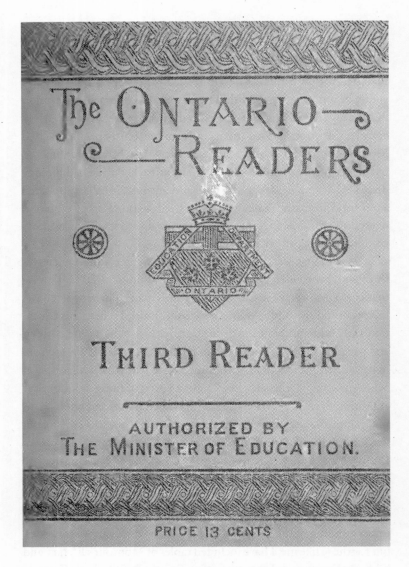

**FIGURE 4.** *The Ontario Readers: Third Reader* (Toronto: W.J. Gage Company, 1885).

While working on the literary references, I learned that many of the poems Montour refers to in *Brown Tom* are also in standard Ontario school textbooks which were likely used in Mount Elgin's classrooms. And sure enough, in some of Montour's editorial notes on his book *The Feathered U.E.L.'s*, he agreed to his editor's suggestion to omit or paraphrase the "Poetry in Chap. 2," explaining, "They 'crept into the Text' on my rewriting. They are from the old Ontario Readers."[7] *Brown Tom* is firmly rooted in Canada's classical (British) curriculum that was part of twentieth-century federal Indian education at Mount Elgin.[8]

In that first online meeting, we identified a path to creating this new edition. Dr. Elizabeth Graham's agreement and contribution were key, as she had taken on the initial editing, typing, and printing of Montour's book, and she writes about that process and the author-editor relationship with Montour in her Foreword to this book. Born in England, Graham herself had attended a boarding school. Cranborne Chase School was a private school for girls in a stately home in Dorset, England. She wanted to become an anthropologist and came to Canada in 1961 to pursue a BA at Trinity College, University of Toronto, and later a Phil M degree in 1967 and a PhD in 1973. Graham published *Brown Tom's Schooldays* in between her own first and second books: *Medicine Man to Missionary: Missionaries as Agents of Change among the Indians of Southern Ontario, 1784–1867* (1975), and *The Mush Hole: Life at Two Indian Residential Schools* (1997).[9] Though each is distinct in form, style, and market, these three works share interesting overlapping themes, including Indian education, Christian mission work, and First Nations histories of southern Ontario.

With Elizabeth's role identified, Mary and Margaret agreed to write about some of their memories of Montour within the context of their lives as his granddaughters. My contribution, it was decided, would be an essay about what we can learn about the history of Mount Elgin from Montour's writing and *Brown Tom's* place within the larger context of Indigenous publishing at the time. Over the next two years, this essay grew substantially as I learned more and more about Montour's life as a student, a United Church minister, a family member, and a member of the Six Nations community from Elizabeth, Margaret, Mary, custodians of the Chapel of the Delaware at Six Nations, Montour's books and articles, and three incredible sets of Montour's correspondence from the 1970s and 1980s. These letters, to Reverend R.C. Plant (Associate Secretary of the Division of Communication at the United Church of Canada [UCC]), United Church missionary Reverend Elgie Ellingham Miller Joblin (who spent many years as a missionary and Day School principal in the Thames River communities), and Dr. Elizabeth Graham, gave me a sense of Montour's commitment to writing and publishing this book. This essay has now shrunk through both condensing and cutting; however, there remains much more to say about Montour and the rich body of work he created. For example, what was his religious writing like? What was his experience of labour within the United Church in the 1930s, '40s, '50s, and '60s? What was his experience of early twentieth-century post-secondary education in Montreal in the 1920s? What analysis can be made of Montour's adaptations of the styles of Charles Dickens and other English and American writers whose work was both a symbol of imperial authority and deeply critical of the limited opportunities available to the poorest of society?

There is also a lot more to learn about the history of Mount Elgin Residential School. How did school life change over time for students? What was Mount Elgin's place within Methodist and United Church social and intellectual circles in southwestern Ontario? How were settler families, farms, and businesses part of the Indian Residential School system? In what ways did student absence from First Nations families put them at a distinct disadvantage during this time of agricultural expansion in this part of Ontario? I am also very interested in the whole and diverse lives of Mount Elgin's graduates, a subject that can be overgeneralized and simplified in some Residential School analyses. As Graham notes in the Foreword to this edition, "any history of Residential Schools is a multi-faceted narrative rooted in its own time and space" (6).

While I was writing drafts of this Introduction, researchers with the Chippewas of the Thames First Nation (COTTFN) were undertaking archival research to learn more about the history of the school so that they could identify students who died at Mount Elgin and attempt to locate where they were buried. The group held a ceremony to open the fieldwork phase, organized a community meeting, and sent letters to the Chiefs of each home community before initiating ground-penetrating radar work on sites associated with Mount Elgin.[10] Another team at COTTFN runs a heritage centre that educates groups, including schoolteachers, about Mount Elgin, and is fundraising to preserve the last remaining building on the Mount Elgin site, a horse barn. The barn is very special because it bears messages and drawings on its walls, carved and written in pen and pencil by students who attended Mount Elgin over the years. The plan is to preserve the barn as a cultural centre that would support and sustain history, language, and cultural learning at COTTFN for years to come.[11] If you would like to donate funds for the project, you can contact the band office.

In the last chapter of *Brown Tom*, Tom and his chums converse about what they want to do after they finish school. Tom states, "Listen you high aimers. Let me tell you about my ambition. I am staying with the books. Books have made me what I am. . . . I want to get my matriculation and 'follow knowledge like a sinking star.'" Enos Montour did just that, and as I followed a trail of his life through the various books, articles, and letters he left behind, I kept coming back to *Brown Tom* as a window into his love of knowledge and his love of books and writing. Elizabeth, Mary, Margaret, and I worked to compile as complete a bibliography of Montour's work as we could, and this is included as Appendix 2.

**FIGURE 5.** Enos Montour, c. 1920. "Enos Montour continued his High School work for several years after leaving the Institute. He is now teaching school. He is an earnest Christian and volunteer for live service. Rev. John Nelson, his present pastor, says, 'We look upon him as one of the coming men of the Six Nations, a typical Canadian, capable of holding a leading position in any community, loyal to and proud of the Institute—his old alma mater.'" The Rev. S.R. McVitty, "Mount Elgin Indian Residential School," *Missionary Bulletin* 16, no. 2 (April–June 1920): 194.

Montour's letters show his understanding of and confidence in his role and authority as author. He was very at home with academics: he was consulted by anthropologist Paul Wallace, and after historian Don Smith asked Montour to review his 1974 thesis, Montour advised that Don needed to put "more raisins in the dough."[12] Montour's letters also evince the relationships he built with those responsible for putting his work out in the world. He cared deeply about those relationships because his writing mattered to him, and he believed it mattered to the world. He was funny and serious and thankful and friendly with those he entrusted with his words. It is difficult to trust someone else with your words—much harder, I imagine, in a world in which Indigenous writers rarely found a place in print, and, when they did, had to navigate relationships with publishers and readers who had a limited and likely oversimplified understanding of Indigenous peoples and history.[13]

## Brown Tom: The Author and the Book

His home at Six Nations, his family and friends, and the church were pillars in Enos Montour's life and writing. Montour was born at Six Nations in 1899 into a Delaware family with a history of Methodist faith and community leadership. Montour's mother died when he was young, and his grandparents raised Enos and his three brothers, Ralph (1897–1975), Moses (1894–1957), and Nathan (1892–1969).[14] Montour left home around 1909 with his older brother Ralph to attend Mount Elgin, but, like many, he maintained strong memories of and connections to home. After reaching Grade 9, Enos attended high school in Hagersville, Ontario. In an interview with the CBC, he explained that he was often identified by teachers, relatives, and others as someone who should be a preacher. He, on the other hand, was modest and self-conscious, and in his own words, he felt like he had been born on the "wrong side of the tracks" for that kind of work.[15]

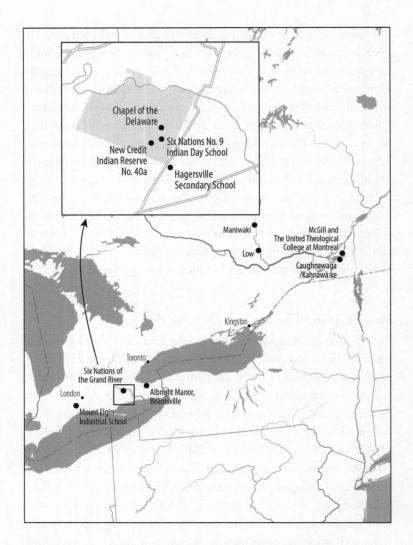

**FIGURE 6.** Map referring to Enos Montour's home community of Six Nations, Mount Elgin, and other places where he received his education. Map by Julie Witmer. Base data © MapTiler © OpenStreetMap contributors.

Montour "ran away" from the church in 1919; even though he already had a job in Hamilton, he went to Toronto and bought a ticket for the Harvest Excursion, a program that brought people to the Canadian West to assist farmers with the grain harvest during the First World War when there was a shortage of farm labour. As Montour recalls, he landed "in the most religious home in the West," where the family said prayers at every meal and had prayer meetings at night. He took this as a sign of his calling. Montour later worked at Six Nations at the end of the war as a day schoolteacher and in farm labour in the Niagara region. At around this time, he was introduced to Dr. Reverend James Smyth (1875–1950). Born in Belfast, Ireland, Smyth moved to Canada in 1911 to take the position of principal of the United Theological College (then called Wesleyan Theological College) and stayed there until 1932, when he retired and returned home. Smyth visited Montour and asked him to enrol at the college that fall, saying, "If you've got the call, we'll put you through. If you haven't, we'll drop you in silence."[16]

A contemporary advertisement for the college in the *Christian Guardian* entitled "Wesleyan Theological College Montreal Prepares Men For The Ministry" described the training as "comprehensive as well as intensive," with courses in arts at McGill University and curriculum in theology that emphasized Bible study and preaching, given by sixteen professors drawn from the Anglican, Congregational, Presbyterian, and Methodist Churches. Theological students were members of the undergraduate body of McGill University and had access to all student activities. "Wesleyan is a residential College," the ad explained. "Here you associate with a great group of men whose aim in life is identical to yours. Daily your ideas and ideals are subjected to their searching analysis and criticism. In them you will find reflected the ideal of Wesleyan, which is to play a leading part in filling our pulpits with strong, well-trained, all-round men."[17] Much of this description might have tempted Brown Tom, the Mount

Elgin student who told his friends he was "staying with the books," and perhaps other aspects of the training, including the religious training and the prospect of living at the college, may have seemed normal and even comfortable.

Nonetheless, few if any of Montour's college friends would be other First Nations men. Work on early Indigenous histories of Canadian and American universities shows that while the education of small numbers of Indigenous students in theology faculties was an important motivation for the founding Canadian universities, a range of barriers meant that Indigenous post-secondary participation overall remained low into the 1980s, when Indigenous efforts to enforce treaty rights to education led to the Post-Secondary Student Assistance Program. Likely none of Montour's professors would have been Indigenous or people of colour, and the United Theological College and McGill more broadly would have, like the Canadian universities studied by Amy Bell, Tom Peace, and Natalie Cross, "played an active transitional role in normalizing a settler presence on Indigenous lands." Photos of Montour in school yearbooks demonstrate networks of missionary families undertaking this work across Canada.[18]

When Montour entered the college in 1921, he expected to go into Home Missions, an evangelical branch of the Methodist Church that encompassed all missions work in Canada, including among Indigenous people. Partway through his training in 1923, as he was doing his senior matriculation to enter McGill, he received a letter from the Home Missions Board. The board said that they were aware that Montour was having a "hard time with his studies and finances"[19] and proposed that he fill a charge in Muskoka where there was a vacancy. The Home Missions Board regularly hired half-trained ministers in its charge when there were not enough ministers to fill the demand. But Montour was advised by the college registrar to decline and to finish his education first so he could "go anywhere." That is what he did. Looking back, Montour explained, "I've been in

**FIGURE 7.** Enos Montour, 1922, probably while working for a farmer during the summer in Horizon, SK while in his Arts Program. Photograph courtesy of Mary I. Anderson and Margaret McKenzie.

French Protestant work, I've been in Indian Work, I've been in the polyglot situation in the West. Just call me 'Mr. Home Mission.'"[20]

In a story about his post-secondary education that Montour hesitated to "tell in public," he recalled a sceptical missionary who came to see Dr. Smyth one day. The missionary said to Dr. Smyth, "You've got this man Montour in there [. . . . S]uppose he finishes his course, and you ordain him. What's going to become of him? There's a man from the bush, he's from the wrong side of the tracks, where will he go?" To this, Dr. Smyth replied, "Look, if Montour turns out to be a cultured

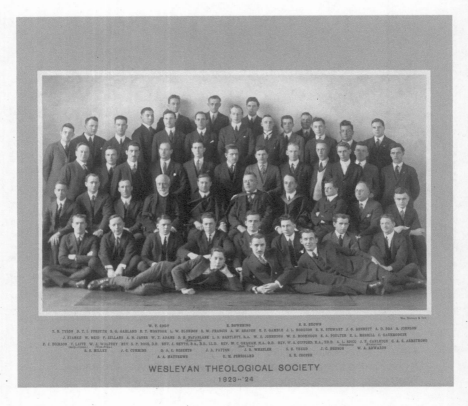

**FIGURE 8.** Wesleyan Theological Society, 1923–1924. McGill University Archives, PL007248.

## ENOS T. MONTOUR

*"This gray spirit yearning in desire to follow knowledge like a sinking star."*

Born July 14, 1900, at Hagersville, Ontario. Attended Hagersville High School. Entered McGill 1923. Winner Neil Stewart Prize in second year. Hobby: *Correspondence.* Favorite expression: *"Is that necessary?"*

ENOS THEODORE
MONTOUR, B.A.

*"Sorrowing, toiling and rejoicing,
Onward through life he goes."*

"The last of the Montours." Born on the banks of the Grand River. Attended High School, Hagersville, Ont. Graduated Arts '27 McGill. Activities: "The Echo" of United College. Executive Theol. Society 1926. Hobby: *Making trips to the Gatineau Valley.* Favourite expression: "*What would you suggest, in a case like that?*"

**FIGURE 9.** Graduation photo of Enos Montour, Bachelor of Arts, 1927 *Old McGill Yearbook*, p. 51.

**FIGURE 10.** Graduation photo of Enos Montour, Bachelor of Divinity 1929 *Old McGill Yearbook*, p. 196.

gentleman, he can go anywhere. If he turns out to be an awkward clod nobody will want him. Not even the Indians."[21]

The Montours' daughter, Shirley McKenzie, married in 1954 and raised her family (including Mary and Margaret) in Aneroid. When Enos Montour retired in 1965, he and his wife moved to Moose Jaw and then to Ponteix, not far from Aneroid, in 1972. After the death of his wife Hilda, Enos moved to the United Church–run retirement home Albright Manor in Beamsville, Ontario, where he met and married his second wife, Florence McNair, BA, a poet and magazine editor from Hamilton and Winnipeg. Here, in a place he called (in his Dickensian way) "the poor house," he completed *Brown Tom's Schooldays* before he died in 1984. Montour is buried in Saskatchewan, where he had lived for a total of thirty-seven years—nearly half of his adult life.

Montour earned a Bachelor of Arts in 1927 and a Bachelor of Divinity with first-class standing in 1929. While a student, Montour served "the steelworking Caughnawaga Indians of Quebec" and directed a multi-denominational and multicultural construction camp church in the power plant boom village of Low in the Gatineau Valley.[22] He was an associate editor of the United Theological College student and alumni newspaper the *Echo*, serving as editor-in-chief in the 1928–29 school year. He was ordained at the age of twenty-nine, on 5 June 1929. That same year, he married Hilda Belle Hanna of Keyes, Manitoba. The Montours then moved to Maniwaki, Quebec, where Montour got his first posting. He wanted to serve First Nations people, but when he applied for an appointment in 1932, "all the missions were occupied" and he worked in Saskatchewan for 14 years before he got back to the Six Nations of the Grand River territory.[23] In the meantime, he worked for about four years each in Ceylon, St. Walburg, Hawarden, and Elrose during the Depression, ministering to mostly White settlers and new immigrants from eastern Canada, the United States, Britain, and Europe.[24]

**FIGURE 11.** Enos Montour loved fishing, but it was Hilda who usually cleaned the fish. Saskatchewan, c. 1950s. Photograph courtesy of Mary I. Anderson and Margaret McKenzie.

FIGURE 12. Enos, Hilda, and Shirley Montour, c. 1950. Photograph courtesy of Mary I. Anderson and Margaret McKenzie.

**FIGURE 13.** Enos and Hilda Montour c. 1950. Photograph courtesy of Mary I. Anderson and Margaret McKenzie.

Montour took his Six Nations roots, his education at Mount Elgin, Hagersville, and McGill, and a flair for writing to churches in these White settler towns. Working as a First Nations ordained United Church preacher on the Prairies would have in turn informed his understanding of Indigenous–Canadian relations and the place that he might find for himself in such a context. In *Brown Tom* he writes about "average Ontario Indian boys"—a subjectivity that was likely informed in part by his experience of living in Saskatchewan. He described "Ontario Indian boys" as being under a lot of pressure to change, as kids who "had not as yet fully adopted the White man's way of life. They were neither fish nor fowl, and in themselves rested the decision as to what they should eventually become" (75). The pressure of having to choose starkly separated Indian or White ways of life was compounded by the association of each with failure or success. A job as a minister to White settlers might have exacerbated other differences between Ontario and the Prairies, including smaller reserves, earlier and more intense settler colonization, and relatively smaller populations of Indigenous people in eastern Canada.

Likewise, the farming knowledge and skills Montour acquired at Mount Elgin and his experience of poverty and hunger there would have shaped his understanding and his practice as a minister in dust-bowl Saskatchewan. For me, Montour's descriptive passages about the outdoor world are like an immediate re-immersion in the leafy, humid life in southwestern Ontario that seems increasingly lush the longer I live in southern Manitoba. Even though he was not itinerant, Montour called himself a "saddlebag preacher";[25] he was also a Six Nations writer living and working in territories where Treaties 4 and 6 had been negotiated within living memory. In Saskatchewan, Montour never worked on or even near a reserve at a time when off-reserve movements of treaty First Nations were still subject to control through social and paralegal practices of racial segregation, including remnants of the pass system—a mechanism instituted in the wake of the 1885 North-West

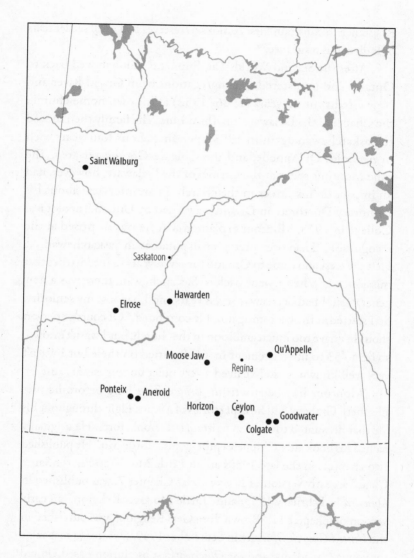

**FIGURE 14.** Map referring to Saskatchewan towns where Enos Montour worked as a minister. Map by Julie Witmer. Base data © MapTiler © OpenStreetMap contributors.

Resistance to constrain First Nations to reserves and quell settler fears of Indigenous resistance.[26]

After the Second World War, Enos and Hilda moved back to Ontario and ministered to congregations from Grand River and New Credit for six years (1946–1952) at his own home church, the Chapel of the Delaware, on Third Line. The family then moved to Saskatchewan again in 1953, spending about four years each in Aneroid, Qu'Appelle, and the Colgate-Goodwater area. The time Montour spent at the Chapel of the Delaware, however, had an impact on his career in the church. In an interview about his Honorary Doctorate in Divinity, awarded by United Theological College in 1975, Montour explained why he was surprised at the recognition. "I had been pretty 'small potatoes' in Saskatchewan.... I left the west and came to Ontario for seven years to reconstruct that mission.... When I went back to Saskatchewan, there was a new generation, I had been away seven years and I had lost my seniority. So I started at the bottom again." He continued, "Of course a person shouldn't have too much ambition in the church, but I wasn't known, so from '53 to my retirement in '65, I carried on there but I wasn't very well-known ... so I've lived a very quiet unobtrusive ... life."[27]

Montour had been writing *Brown Tom* long before he met Elizabeth Graham, and he kept stories of Mount Elgin throughout his life that he wanted to share in written, later book, form. He originally named his book after Chippewa protagonist "Little Mo." He published two chapters in the late 1950s about Little Mo: "Too Big for Santa Claus," an early version of *Brown Tom's* Chapter 7, was published in *Onward* in February 1958; and "Little Mo Gets Religion," an early version of Chapter 11, "Brown Tom Gets Religion," was published in the *United Church Observer* in September 1959. *Onward* (a magazine for young Canadians) and the *Observer* (a subscription-based United Church magazine) were two of the many publications of the United Church Publishing House.[28]

24

Montour's work was produced within a network of United Church journalism and publishing, but he wrote for a broader public outside of the church market as well. This dichotomy led to some back-and-forth for Montour, whose social network included not only church publishers but also Canadian and American scholars, writers, and journalists, and family and friends. He waffled on the best home for his books—a mainstream Canadian publisher or the United Church Publishing House—based on available opportunities, trends in publishing at the time, and his comfort with editors who represented publishers. His first book, *The Feathered U.E.L.'s* (1973), was sponsored in part by a Canada Council grant under its Canadian Horizons program and published by the Division of Communication of the United Church (later known as the United Church Publishing House). *The Feathered U.E.L.'s* was distributed by the United Church and by Montour himself, who placed bulk orders through the distributor, CANEC, in Don Mills, Ontario. Reverend R.C. "Bob" Plant, who had training as a journalist as well as a preacher and was secretary of the Committee on Education for Mission and Stewardship in the Division of Congregational Life, was a valuable partner in Montour's efforts to publish.[29] At this time, there was a mix of both secular and sacred texts published by the United Church.[30] Montour's *The Feathered U.E.L.'s* was a book about Delaware history at Six Nations, not a religious text; however, it might have fit the sacred division's list because its author was a minister and because of Montour's relationship with Plant. Available for sale at Eaton's department store and at Canada Drug and Book Company, *The Feathered U.E.L.'s* sold well, was reviewed in newspapers across the country, and achieved three print runs. Montour's honorary doctorate was awarded in part because of the book.

The years between *The Feathered U.E.L.'s* and *Brown Tom* (from 1973 to 1985) are significant to the history of the book in Canada: awareness of and demand for books about Indigenous people rose among Canadian readers, and small, medium, and large Canadian presses worked to feed these audiences.[31] Biography, memoir, and other life writing was a particularly successful genre within this wave. In one letter sent to R.C. Plant in 1973, Montour enclosed a page from a recent issue of the Indian Affairs' newspaper, *Indian News*, advertising a selection of new First Nations literature. The image featured twenty-one titles arranged around a message from the *Indian News* editor: "Best Wishes ... from *The Indian Bookshelf*" (Figure 15, ellipses in original).[32] Montour added in the margins, "Injun Writers and white publishers—latest list—they're coming out of the bush."[33] This short list of publications (see Table 1) shows a slight bias toward First Nations men writers (four) over First Nations women writers (three), but a more pronounced bias of men writers and editors (eleven) over women (seven). This gender bias reflects the Canadian publishing industry at the time.[34]

This list also shows a trend for Indigenous authors to produce books in partnership with non-Indigenous anthropologists or sociologists. Graham was an anthropologist, but she was not an "as told to" collaborator in the making of *Brown Tom*. Reverend Elgie E.M. Joblin (1909–1993) was another partner with whom Montour worked in his writing. Joblin had been a missionary at Oneida of the Thames First Nation in the 1930s and was the principal of Mount Elgin Residential and later Day School in the 1940s and '50s, after which he took on administrative roles in the Home Missions branch of the United Church. Joblin communicated with Montour on several occasions in the 1970s, including in his role of creating a training textbook for church missionaries and in his efforts to write his own book on Indigenous priests and ministers in Canada. In letters to R.C. Plant and Elgie Joblin, Montour began talking about "book 2," his "End book," which would focus on his years at Mount Elgin. In 1970 he sent Joblin a draft table of contents of "an 8 spasm account of Mt Elgin life, from the inside."[35] One chapter, "Little Mo Finds Life's

Page Twelve 'INJUN' Writers & white Publishers THE INDIAN NEWS November - December/Novembre - Décembre, 1972

*latest list* *& those coming out of the Bush* JAN 22 1973

*Best Wishes... from The Indian Bookshelf*

Design by: *Don Konrad*

Photo Credit: *Bill Badcock*

**SECRET IN THE STLALAKUM WILD by Christie Harris**
The author of RAVEN'S CRY, one of the best books in the Indian literature series, has come out with another book combining the Northwest and the Indians. 'Stlalahums are unnatural beings in the natural world. To the Old Coast Salish Indians, they were an explanation for many strange events." These lines challengingly invite readers of all ages to explore the Northwest coast world through SECRET IN THE STLALAHUM WILD.
Atheneum Publishers, New York City, $4.95.

* * *

**RECOLLECTIONS OF AN ASSINIBOINE CHIEF by Dan Kennedy (Ochankugahe)**
Dan Kennedy is over 100 years old and recounts the history of his people, indeed of life in early Saskatchewan, in this fine book. If Canada has witnessed tremendous changes in the country over the past 100 years, so too has Dan Kennedy. Many historic moments are recorded in his book.
Toronto and Montreal, $7.95 McClelland and Stewart,

* * *

**TALES FROM THE IGLOO** edited and translated by Maurice

Metayer with illustrations by Agnes Nanogak.
An intriguing look into Eskimo culture. TALES FROM THE IGLOO, is not only fascinating in content but in illustrations as well. The book contains 22 legends of the Copper Eskimos which have been passed down by word of mouth. The legends give the world phenomenons a meaning and a source.
Hurtig Publishers, Edmonton, $4.95

* * *

**A SMALL AND CHARMING WORLD by John Frederic Gibson**
Written with an insight often lacking in civil servants, Mr. Gibson's book is the most compassionate and thoughtful piece of literature dealing with Indians to appear in a long time. The author writes with a decided air of authenticity and understanding of a way of like known to too few non-Indians, and has managed to produce an altogether delightful narrative. Should be required reading for all government field-workers who have contact with native people.
Collins Press, Toronto and London $6.95

**NATIVE RIGHTS IN CANADA** (2nd Edition) — edited by P. A.

Cumming and N. H. Mickenberg. Twice the length of the first edition of 1970, this second edition of NATIVE RIGHTS IN CANADA is *the* source book for anyone interested in the legal aspects of injustice to native people. It examines the question of aboriginal rights from both a national and international point of view, and deals with both status and non-status Indians and Eskimos. An excellent reference work.
General Publishing, Toronto, $7.95 (pb)

* * *

**GREAT LEADER OF THE OJIBWAY: MIS-QUONA-QUEB by James Redsky**
The exploits of the last great war leader of the Ojibway as told by James Redsky from stories he heard in his childhood some seventy years ago. Includes descriptions of the Ojibway religion, the society of medicine men, the shaking tent, and a way of life that has all but vanished.
McClelland and Stewart, Toronto, $7.95

* * *

**TALES OF NOKOMIS by Patronella Johnston**
Patronella Johnston, an Ojibway from the Cape Croker Reserve in Ontario, has written these legends of her people as a measure to preserve the Indian culture and to teach young people. Colour illustrations by Francis Kagige.
Chales J. Musson, Ltd., Toronto.

* * *

**SONGS OF THE DREAM PEOPLE by James Houston**
Chants and images of the Indians and Eskimos of North America written and illustrated by James Houston. Drawings of art objects and weapons coupled with songs of America's First People.
Atheneum New York, $5.95

* * *

**I AM AN INDIAN** edited by Kent Gooderham
The first anthology of Indian literature published in Canada; written and illustrated by Sioux, Salish, Ojibway, Delaware Abnakis and Assiniboine men and women. J. M. Dent & Sons (Canada) Ltd., Toronto.

* * *

**AN INDIAN REMEMBERS by Tom Boulanger**
Told in diary-like style, Tom Boulanger relates his life as a trapper in northern Manitoba. To obtain an insight into the life of Indian people since the turn of the century in northern Manitoba, AN INDIAN REMEMBERS is definitely a valuable source.
Peguis Publishers, Winnipeg, $4.95

**FIGURE 15.** *Indian News*, November–December 1972, 12, with Montour's marginalia across the top. 22 January 1973, Letter to Plant from Montour Enos T. Montour Fonds, 1986.25C, File 1, United Church of Canada Archives.

TABLE 1. *INDIAN NEWS* BOOKS*

| Title | Info | Publisher | Date |
|---|---|---|---|
| *Sepass Poems: The Songs of Y-Ail Mihth* | Songs by (Salish Chief) William K'H Halserten recorded by non-Indigenous poet Eloise Street. | Vantage Press | 1963 |
| *White Sioux: Major Walsh of the Mounted Police* | A book about North-West Mounted Police officer James Morrow Walsh, by non-Indigenous author Iris Allan. | Gray's Publishing | 1969 |
| *I Am Indian* | An anthology of First Nations literature, edited by non-Indigenous anthropologist, educator, and Indian Affairs civil servant Kent Gooderham, aka George Kentner Gooderham. | J.M. Dent | 1969 |
| *Guests Never Leave Hungry* | An autobiography of Kwakiutl Chief James Sewid, edited by non-Indigenous anthropologist James P. Spradley. | Yale University Press | 1969 |
| *Tawow* | An Indigenous cultural periodical, edited by Six Nations Mohawk Mary Jamieson. | Indian Affairs | 1970–1981 |
| *Tales of Nokomis* | An autobiography by Cape Croker Ojibway writer Verna Patronella Johnson. | Charles J. Musson | 1970 |
| *Money of the American Indians* | A book by non-Indigenous American numismatist and historian Don Taxay. | Nummus Press | 1970 |
| *An Indian Remembers* | An autobiography by Oxford House Cree trapper Tom Boulanger. | Peguis Publishers | 1971 |

| | | | |
|---|---|---|---|
| *Forbidden Voice: Reflections of a Mohawk* | An autobiography by Six Nations Mohawk healer and community leader Alma Greene, Gah-wonh-nos-doh. | Hamlyn Publishing Group | 1971 |
| *Native Rights in Canada*, 2nd ed. | An edited collection by non-Indigenous law professors Peter Cumming and Neil Mickenberg. | Indian-Eskimo Association of Canada | 1972 |
| *A Small and Charming World* | A book by non-Indigenous civil servant and writer John Frederic Gibson. | Collins Press | 1972 |
| *Secret in the Stlalakum Wild* | A book by non-Indigenous author Christie Harris. | Athenium | 1972 |
| *Songs of the Dream People* | A book edited by non-Indigenous civil servant, artist, and writer James Houston. | Longman | 1972 |
| *Recollections of an Assiniboine Chief* | An autobiography of Carry-the-Kettle Nakoda Chief Dan Kennedy, aka Ochankugahe, edited by James R. Stevens. | McClelland and Stewart | 1972 |
| *Tales from the Igloo* | A book edited by non-Indigenous Oblate missionary Maurice Métayer. | Hurtig Publishers | 1972 |
| *The American Indian Craft Book* | A book by non-Indigenous writers and photographers Marz and Nono Minor. | Popular Library | 1972 |
| *Great Leader of the Ojibway: Mis-Quona-Queb* | An autobiography of Lake of the Woods area Ojibway leader James Redsky, aka Esquekesik, edited by James R. Stevens. | McClelland and Stewart | 1972 |
| *Potlatch* | A book by Tseshaht artist, actor, and writer George Clutesi. | Gray's Publishing | 1973 |

\* This table represents books shown in *Indian News*, November–December 1972, 12.

Work," did not make it into *Brown Tom*. This chapter was described in the contents as "Across the Anglin' Trails—Dead Mans Hill at Midnight—Strange Calls on the Prairie Breeze."[36]

He wrote again to Joblin in 1973:

> I'd like your personal opinion on an idea I've been toying with. [arrow] Do you think the H.M. [Home Missions] Board would be interested in preserving an account of life in an Indian boarding school? Would they sponsor my effort in the same way the Canada Council did with my first book [*The Feathered U.E.L.'s*]? If the answer is yes, to whom would I write? Of course you would never be quoted. I've been thinking of the secular market with Dent or Gage publishers but my friends tell me this is a subject that has never been written about so I thought the church might be interested.[37]

In 1975 Montour sent Joblin a fifteen-chapter table of contents and the manuscript for "The Burning of the Barns," which later became Chapter 9 of *Brown Tom*, "Trial by Fire." Montour had heard that the Home Missions Board of the UCC was interested in "preserving an account of life as it was lived in these Church Boarding Schools."[38]

But while Montour sought out sponsorship from the UCC's Home Missions Board, he also considered the "secular market" as an appropriate place for *Brown Tom*.[39] He contemplated school text and dictionary publisher Gage and educational publisher Clarke Irwin, both eventually purchased by Nelson, a major educational publisher. He also mulled over Dent, best known for their Everyman's Library series. In a letter to Graham, referenced in her Foreword, Montour explained that his book would help to address the contemporary demand for books on Indian Residential Schools and pointed to a recent story covered by Johnny Yesno on his CBC Winnipeg show

*Our Native Land*, which discussed the discovery of a "detention hole (dungeon) into which difficult urchins were thrown."[40] This dungeon, found in the Mohawk Institute when the Woodland Indian Centre took over the buildings in the 1980s, is a reminder of the punitive discipline used with children at Indian Residential Schools that would have been familiar to Montour.

Montour felt that the church publishing market might be more receptive to his book but insisted that his work about Mount Elgin was not "a solely Missionary Project."[41] At the same time, he seemed uncertain about the fit of his style with the secular market for Indigenous-authored books. In his correspondence with friends, Montour wondered if his writing was perhaps overlooked because it did not meet the expectations of readers. When sales of his *The Feathered U.E.L.'s* lagged behind expectations, he jealously pointed to the success of Maria Campbell's *Halfbreed*, published by McClelland and Stewart.[42] In 1974, he learned that Dent Publishers in Toronto had offered to read anything sent to them by the director of the Woodland Indian Cultural Centre, Glenn Crain. Montour sent Crain four chapters of what would become *Brown Tom*,[43] but by August 1975, Dent had still not returned his chapters and Montour seemed concerned his book would not be judged to appeal to the market. Montour wrote to Plant about publishers' possible indictment, "Author seems to know so little of sex and 4 letter words."[44] Later that month, Dent publishers returned the sample chapters. "Too mild, too innocent, out of touch with modrn [*sic*] realities. Erf," Montour wrote Plant. He also noted that "they seem rather disorganized at Dent. The chap who agreed to read whatever Director Crain of the Indian Cultural centre, Brantford sent them is 'not with Dent any more.'" He also noted that a few items from his original submission were missing from the returned manuscript.[45]

At around this time, Montour sometimes referred to himself as "Lone Eagle" or "Dr Lone Eagle" in his correspondence with Plant, perhaps humorously asserting a role in both Indigenous and White worlds while simultaneously pointing out the inadequacy of flimsy binary representations to fully represent his voice. At the same time, the ucc's Division of Mission declined to subsidize Montour's second book, then titled "Feathered Urchins at Boarding School."[46] Despite connections with Joblin and Plant, and without funding from Canada Council or elsewhere, the ucc did not agree to support the publishing of the book.

At some point, Montour obtained a brochure for Pathway Publications in Toronto, which, for $100, would review a manuscript and if approved, would publish, print, promote, and distribute it. Pathway, Montour explained to Graham, was "interested in 'Christian' writers and their products. That means no 4 letter words." Montour said he was going to send them an introduction and a copy of his "Loyalists book."[47] By April 1983, however, Pathway was no longer in business and Montour was struggling to find a quiet, comfortable place to work and dealing with increasing aches and pains. He wrote to Graham, "Until you hear from me again, please forget me and my unfinished project." In May of that year, he wrote, "There is just one more alternative left to us re: Brown Tom's School Days. Have it photocopied and be done with it."[48]

Too often, Indigenous writers are depicted as or assumed to be novices, as strangers to using pen and paper to communicate. When he wrote *Brown Tom*, Montour was not "finding his voice." He had spent his career writing sermons—short, instructive stories and lessons for a broad, if captive, audience. Over the years he had also written short, popular-interest pieces for local newspapers, including McGill's *College Magazine*, the United Theological College's *The Echo*, the *Hamilton Spectator*, the *Regina Leader-Post*, and the *Brantford Expositor*. He had graduated from a program with the Newspaper Institute of America and was on the executive of the Canadian Authors Association. In a letter to Graham, he wrote, "I was District

Reporter for Brantford Expositor in the '50s. My Supe used to say 'I want 1,000 words on "Indian Snow Snake."' I had no trouble in providing Copy. So the same procedure can get me furiously writing in '82."[49] As Graham points out in her Foreword to this volume, Montour vetted her as an editor in their early correspondence and had done his research on whom he would be working with, a smart move many writers might not consider when choosing a publisher. He was aware of publishing currents and had carefully considered the market, sales potential, and readership for his book.

Montour wanted a publisher that would document and amplify his voice, but presses like Dent fed a reading public that expected Indigenous literature to deliver essentialized, gritty, and dramatic depictions of Indian life. In the 1970s, there were a few books about life in Indian Residential Schools, mostly from women's perspectives,[50] while men's memoirs tended to focus on other content such as cultural heritage and political writing on Indian policy, anti-Indigenous racism, and inequality in Canada. Starting in the 1980s, there was a rise of both Indigenous men's and women's life writing on Residential Schooling, most notably Basil Johnston's *Indian School Days* (1988). None of these books dealt with Mount Elgin; remarkably, given the size and length of operation of the school, *Brown Tom* remains to my knowledge the only published life-writing on Mount Elgin.

Haudenosaunee literary scholar Rick Monture's careful analysis of *The Feathered UEL's* is very helpful to understanding Montour's writing in *Brown Tom*.[51] Monture acknowledges Montour's position as a Christian and a loyalist and contextualizes his detached portrayal of the assimilationist agenda of Mount Elgin. For example, while discussing the future with a friend near the end of his time at Mount Elgin, Brown Tom says, "I'm not going to be like other folks when I get back to the Reserve. It's awful how ignorant some of them are" (76). A reader today might flinch at that statement, especially coming from an Indigenous

**FIGURE 16.** Enos Montour, press photo for *The Feathered U.E.L.'s*. United Church of Canada Archives, 76.001 P4091.

character, and indeed Brown Tom's friend "stirred annoyedly" (76) but did not interject. Montour's use of the word "swarthy" (74) to describe Tom and other First Nations people also leans into racist stereotypes. At the same time, though, the book's title makes race an inescapable element of the book: *this* Tom was brown-skinned, as opposed to his White, English predecessor, Tom Brown.

Thomas Hughes's 1857 classic *Tom Brown's School Days* depicts the life of an English boy at Rugby School, an elite private boarding school for older boys and the birthplace of rugby football. It is considered a founding text of muscular Christianity, a Victorian ideal that celebrated physical athleticism, patriotic duty, and self-sacrifice as appropriate characteristics of moral men. *Tom Brown* "marked the starting point" of the school story genre of youth fiction, which centred on older pre-adolescent and adolescent life, most commonly at English private schools.[52] Montour's *Brown Tom* and Hughes's *Tom Brown* have several similarities beyond their titles and institutional settings. Both combine fictional and non-fictional elements based on the authors' experiences at school and cover themes of school events, bullying, friendship, growing up, and learning about one's position within a larger community. The title of Montour's book about an "Ojibwa boy" at Mount Elgin gives you a sense of the brilliance of his writing. The title is a "dad joke," Monture has observed,[53] that is like an open door to an era and a style of humour that for us may be a few generations removed but remains remarkably familiar. As Enos Montour explained to one journalist in 1981, it is a "play on words with an ethnic twist on the famous *Tom Brown's School Days*."[54] Today, it pokes holes in the false comparisons made by Residential School denialists between boarding schools and Indian Residential Schools.[55]

What does it mean to call someone "Brown Tom" in a context of violent cultural assimilation and dispossession amid a profound denial of the same? Rick Monture suggests that Montour uses stereotypes to present an interpretation of the past that is "more agreeable to the casual reader, and not necessarily one intended for a [First Nations] audience."[56] One might also wonder, however, what the flipped name in the title means for the rest of the book, and how we might approach the ostensibly simple tale of a boy at boarding school. I would argue that Enos Montour also wrote for a senior sector of the First Nations community, people who had attended Residential Schools in the early twentieth century and understood the context (metaphors, jokes, and poetry) better than we do. These First Nations readers endured, experienced, and incorporated to varying degrees the assimilatory training and effects of Indian Residential Schools; they too had faced limited choices after finishing school. These readers likely also enjoyed Montour's clever facility with the literary canon and the way Montour handles the book's more humorous and serious moments.

The title can be interpreted as a gift of wit in a difficult context and a pointed dig at the Indian Department and how it treats First Nations people. It also sets the tone for a book by an educated, well-read, and gifted writer. Innocent stories can hide a terrible and complex reality of marginalization, loneliness, anti-Indigenous racism, fear, and loss. Inuk literary scholar Kristina Fagan argues that storytelling can be a way to "bare the unbearable and thus to survive." In *Brown Tom*, Montour underscores rather than conceals his "four years of hunger" at Mount Elgin, documenting and sharing the experience to deal with it. Fagan argues that writers use storytelling to explore connections between "the traumatic past and troubles in the present and to self-reflexively examine the potential and limits of such indirect and humorous communication."[57] Daniel Heath Justice argues that Indigenous stories can both wound and heal; and "give shape, substance, and purpose to our existence and help us understand how to uphold our responsibilities to one another and the rest of creation, especially in places and times so deeply affected by colonial fragmentation. . . . [T]hey tell the truths of our presence in the world today, in days past, and in days to come." Indigenous stories, Justice claims, respond to core questions about Indigenous belonging, identities, and relationships, including one that I think that Montour's works address: "How do we learn to live together?" Montour describes "Three Worlds" that Tom grapples with, each with its own intellectual and cultural structures and conventions: the first (his Home Reserve), the second (White Man's World) and the third—the world of the Residential School. Montour's stories richly describe these worlds and their differences, and reflect on conflict and harmonious relations within and between them.[58] Composed in bits and pieces over forty years and prioritized only at the end of his

"Feathered Urchins at Boarding School"
(The Adventures of "Little 'Mo.)

Chap 1 - "The Green and Salad Days" The Privileged Years
of Sr. Boys Grade 8.
" 2. "Trials of a "New Boy"
" 3. "Loaf 'n' Lard" (10¢ "Feasts"- always hungry
" 4 The milling Herd - Variety Reserves and Dialects
" 5. Little 'Mo makes a Deal - (Heel of Bread for Sunday Cake"
Securing their Birthrights)
" 6 Too Big for Santa Claus - (Little 'Mo's Dark Hour)
" 7. Tread by Fire (Burning of School Barns)
" 8 Puppy Love in the "Mush-Hole"
(Little 'Mo "Has It Bad")
" 9. Roar of mighty Waters (Spring Floods)
" 10 Little 'Mo Gets Religion (church vs Longhouse)
" 11. "Happy Hunting Ground" via TB (Consumption
(wherein we lose a boy)
" 12. Little 'Mo's Three Worlds - (Bush/City) School)
" 13 War Clouds over Mt Oliver (The Boys "Over There"
" 14 Little 'Mo's "Happy Days" (Happy to get back
to school)
" 15 A Strange Graduation - (The Sr. Class has a
last Confab.)

E.T.M.

**FIGURE 17.** Draft Table of Contents for *The Feathered Urchins at Boarding School (The Adventures of Little 'Mo)*. Note in Chapter 13, Mount Elgin is referred to as "Mt Oliver" after Strapp. Letter to R.C. Plant from Montour, n.d., c. late 1975, Enos T. Montour Fonds, 1986.258C, File 2, United Church of Canada Archives.

life after writing two other books, *Brown Tom* was likely a lot more difficult to write, and then let go of, than we will ever know.

Importantly, Rick Monture does not present Montour's work as simply "colonized" and essentially "non-Native." Rather, he shows that Montour's work itself is not irreconcilable with Longhouse religion and Confederacy governance at Six Nations. He also argues that Montour's use of stereotypes does not mean that he fails to see wider cultures of racism and prejudice that regularly impact First Nations people's lives and opportunities. Indeed, to use them is to know them. In his hokey, uplifting, celebratory review of the old days, Montour in fact humorously opposes what most people in the early 1970s might have assumed about Indigenous people. Moreover, he represented the past through the eyes of a successful graduate of the school while discreetly making room for the more serious traumas readers may have endured. Rick Monture counts Montour's work within a literary movement to decolonize First Nations and empower communities. At the same time, Enos Montour was an integral part of a web of scholars studying imperialism, Christianity, and Anishinaabe and Haudenosaunee history in southern Ontario. Ironically, at the time and even much later, predominantly White settler historians considered the writings of Indigenous historians to be "polemic" and "lacking objectivity," and thus not truly scholarly.[59] Indeed, Montour's writing remains highly relevant today.

In some ways it is remarkable that the book ever made it out into the wider world. Its latter stages of preparation coincided with considerable change for Montour. His wife of forty years, Hilda (his "Irish rose"), had passed away of cancer in 1974, and he moved from Saskatchewan to Albright Manor in Ontario, where he met his second wife, Florence. He was writing *The Rockhound of New Jerusalem*, his biography of Gilbert Montour, and consulting with relatives as well as with provincial and federal government officials and civil servants. While his writing is clear, he struggled with cataracts, a hernia, and leg pain, among other ailments, making both writing and typing difficult. He wrote to Plant in 1976: "'Cataract' eyes need guideline so my Olivetti 45 [typewriter] is having a rest."[60] In 1983, he wrote Graham that "I have one good eye (cataract op.): one fair ear, [?] deafness. I balance myself by grasping the nearest ladies arm. Oh yes, Hernia and Arthritis. Apart from all these I am in fairly good shape."[61] His determination to finish the manuscript, especially during this period of his life, is moving and makes *Brown Tom* even more valuable.

Although he clearly wanted to write and pull his work together, he complained to Graham about not being able to "depend on Craft Room to work in—too many special events there. No place here where I can settle down comfortably to write. There are too many Manor events breaking into my writing chore.... What's more Gramp has had too many Birthdays I guess. So many aches and pains.... I've had to give up typing. Will send you (sometime) rewritten long-hand sample chapters." It is clear he was frustrated with his "unfinished project."[62] Hernia surgery put him in a wheelchair for a while, at which point he chose to go the route of photocopying his book. By then, the project was entirely in Graham's hands to "carry the ball."[63] Close to the end, Montour wrote to Graham, "You did a splendid job in turning out "Brown Tom's School Days"—I wasn't of much help at the time. Please send me a copy as soon as issued."[64]

That the book was not professionally published seems an important attribute to consider. While Enos's deteriorating health ultimately forced his and Graham's decision to self-publish, the relationships he had built with editors and academics had failed to yield encouragement from a publisher. The Royal Commission on Aboriginal Peoples (1996) noted that it was nearly sixty years after poet Pauline Johnson's death in 1913 before Indigenous authors would reappear on Canada's literary scene. Without the support and interest of a predominantly non-Indigenous, male mainstream publishing industry, Indigenous writers and others made knowledge more widely available by self-publishing limited-run "grey literature," much of which, unfortunately, rather quickly became difficult to locate and access. *Brown Tom* was published within what some literary experts have called "printing cultures" (as distinguished from "large scale and authoritative public texts of 'print culture'"), which were "small-scale and localized, serving the needs of particular families or individuals"[65] but also highly responsive to the lived realities of Indigenous expression within colonizing nations.

The technology of copying, first by Gestetner machine and then by photocopier, was part of the culture of Indigenous literature and politics in the twentieth century. A Gestetner was a hand-cranked or electric machine with an inking roller and a stencil made up of a waxy sheet attached at the top by a stiff edge to a backing sheet. One would feed this stencil into a typewriter until it was in position and type onto the waxy sheet with the backing behind it; for illustrations, you could use a stylus to draw on the waxy sheet. This created the "original" to be duplicated. After applying a thin coating of Gestetner ink (which lasted for a surprising number of copies per application) to the inking roller, one would apply the wax stencil (without the backing) to it. Cranking the machine rotated the ink drum, fed the paper in, and pressed it over the stencil and roller, forcing the ink through onto the paper. Over time, processes such as inking were made more automated in some models, but the principle remained the same.

The Gestetner could be messy and required familiarity with the machine and its temperament. By the 1980s, when *Brown Tom* was published, one could go to a print shop with an original hard copy, or even a computer disk, that would be placed in a machine by a shop worker who could print any number of copies of the whole document by pressing a button. Increasingly, one could find photocopiers for use by customers directly, even at corner shops, that were programmed to charge by the page. From school assignments to business and government correspondence, to newsletters by social and political organizations, as well as books and pamphlets, documents generated via these mechanisms account for a substantial measure of the literature by and about Indigenous people and history from this era that we still retain. When researching and learning about Indigenous literary history, we do well to look beyond the published book or poem to collections of Indigenous archives across the country.

## Autobiography, Fiction, Evidence

One reason for *Brown Tom*'s omission from mainstream Canadian publishing markets was that it did not fit expectations for First Nations life writing, being partly fictionalized and drawing so heavily on English literary devices and classic works. At the same time, it is based solidly in a real place and draws from lived First Nations experiences, not from expected and well-worn "Indian" tropes, but set in a nineteenth-century English school genre. Yet the central tension in the book is specific to First Nations people, for whom survival meant not simply moving confidently toward adulthood by taking on middle-class values but also learning self-doubt and prejudice before facing a choice for a White or an Indian future world, each with its own comforts and perils. It is likely that much of this escaped publishers and editors looking for more explicitly blunt and unpolished descriptions of Indigenous trauma that would be read as "true" non-fiction.

Still, thirty years after *Brown Tom* was put into print, it is cited in the Final Report of the Truth and Reconciliation Commission (TRC) for its descriptions of perpetual hunger and a student's death from tuberculosis, its explanation of the day-to-day discouragement of Indian languages at Mount Elgin, and its discussion of the impact of the First World War on race relations in Residential Schools. The TRC report also points to the "devastating end" of *Brown Tom*, when teachers question the usefulness of the school itself: "Had this all been a mistake? Had these gifts not only served to unfit them for the old

Reserve life without being able to promise them very much out in the great big Anglo-Saxon world? Had it been for better or worse?" (152)[66] That Montour uses *Brown Tom* to express his impression of teachers' self-doubts is a brilliant literary device that highlights the frail but violent core of the Indian Residential School system and the broader Canadian society it reflected.

Should readers think of *Brown Tom* as historical evidence? Fiction? Memoir? As a historian, I am prone to think about memoirs not as a genre but as a source. Especially in the field of Indigenous history, where sources about our past are overwhelmingly non-Indigenous and few deal with life history, books like *Brown Tom* are valuable, teachable primary sources. Further, I work in a field that still too often assumes that authentic Indigenous knowledge is only orally transmitted[67] and that Indigenous written sources, when they are acknowledged, lack credibility. Literary scholars have identified and described Indigenous textual cultures in ways that can help understand Montour's work from other perspectives. Tony Ballantyne and Lachy Paterson's edited collection offers insights into how *Brown Tom* was produced within dynamics of Indigenous communication, community, and imperial engagement and contestation.[68] They also push scholars to think about how Montour's writing skilfully references British, American, and biblical textual cultures in a story that addresses the struggle of adolescence, institutional education, and modern Indigenous relations in the context of an aggressive push to terminate Indigenous rights in twentieth-century Canada. Montour's upturning of Thomas Hughes's popular classic *Tom Brown's School Days* digs right into this modern Indigenous social and cultural production and asserts, as Ballantyne and Paterson explain, "intellectual power within the uneven cultural terrains created by colonial rule."[69]

One of the many reasons I find *Brown Tom's Schooldays* fascinating is that while it ironically references privileged British schooling at the height of empire, it is concretely linked with very real places, people, and events in early twentieth-century southwestern Ontario First Nations. As in *Tom Brown*, the book's fictional elements include allusions to classical literature evoked and intended as "universal" cultural tropes. As the only substantive writing I have found by a student at Mount Elgin during this time period, *Brown Tom* perhaps stands as weightier historical evidence than it was ever intended to be. It was written "after the fact"—the earliest chapters were first published in the 1950s, about forty years after Montour left Mount Elgin and completed after a long career in the United Church. He left no obvious guide in the book to help readers decipher what and who is true to Mount Elgin's lived history; perhaps he intended to talk about this after the book was published, or perhaps he was content that his schoolmates and other "insiders" would recognize themselves in the book. But for me, as an outsider looking back and as a historian, Montour left a veritable buffet of breadcrumbs to follow, and I regularly reflect on and rely on the book to link and illuminate the intellectual and social histories of First Nations of Ontario in the early decades of the twentieth century.

With the exception of the barn, there are no remaining Mount Elgin School and farm buildings and only a few accessible historical photos to help understand what it looked like. Mount Elgin's main, four-storey building sat on a bank above the Thames River, and it is identified and described in the first chapter as it is seen "looming in the distance" by Brown Tom and his friend from a boat (75). Elizabeth Graham writes that Mount Elgin's buildings symbolized "grand ideas of the munificence of Church or Government, but the condition in which the buildings were maintained represented the value society put on their use . . . and how the occupants were viewed."[70] The Victorian architecture matched the school staff, who, as Montour explains, were "recruited from the Anglo-Saxon world" (75) and were trained "scholars or workmen" (75). During Montour's time there, the teaching staff was overwhelmingly from the United Kingdom, including the "Irish principal," the "English lady" (103), the "Belfast minister" (120), the "Irish Stockman" (121), and the local minister, a "son o' Glasgae" (133). Staff members were hired by the church and paid by the federal government to train the children in Christianity, industry, and farming. Their goal was to teach and discipline young First Nations people to assimilate according to the ideals of Protestant Christianity and the Department of Indian Affairs, and ultimately to eliminate Indigenous nations, cultures, and languages. Chronic and intentional parsimony of both church and department made the industrial school unsafe, impoverished, and stressful.

Inadequate funding led to poorly maintained infrastructure, buildings, staffing, diet, and clothing. The use of unpaid student labour to compensate the school's meagre resources meant that academic schooling was provided for only a few hours of the day. Mount Elgin, like many of the older Indian Residential Schools, was not originally intended to be managed this way. Anishinaabe nations of southern Ontario provided the land and funding to build and establish the school in the early nineteenth century as equal partners with church and government. However, by the time the school opened in 1851, First Nations involvement had been radically cut out of the nascent Residential School system, as churches and government put overall and day-to-day decision-making powers in the hands of Indian Affairs education branch officials in Ottawa, Indian agents locally, and clergy hired by the churches. Resistance to this structure by parents and students was consistent and significant, ranging from large-scale efforts like lawsuits and petitions to Parliament to everyday acts like stealing food and running away.[71]

Between the 1850s and the 1940s, life around the institution changed considerably. It was an era of "progress" in Canada, often celebrated in history texts as the "National Era," when the country coalesced and prospered economically through agriculture and industrialization. Politically, First Nations were to have little to no role in the newly formed nation-state of Canada, despite their considerable and consistent efforts. Rather, the 1876 Indian Act fashioned members of sovereign First Nations as individual "wards" of the federal government until they integrated into the national fabric. In this vision, an individual's success was tied to their British citizenship and associated with their contributions to capitalism, Christianity, and Canadian nation building. At the schools, the stated thrust of education for First Nations children was to prepare them to take their place as domestic and farm help to White settler families in Canadian town and country life.

Students at the school did not miss this crucial subtext of their curriculum. Montour writes of the two distinct, mutually exclusive, and not particularly attractive choices Residential School students faced:

> graduates had only been brought to the parting of
> the ways. The school could lead them no further, nor
> advise them which road to take. The one road was an
> unpromising but familiar and well-worn one. It led back
> to the Reserve life. The other was a bright upland way, but
> beset by many uncertainties. It led out to the great Anglo-
> Saxon world of competition and continuous struggle.
>
> There were two lions at the gateway of this latter road.
> The one was subjective, the other objective. They were an
> inferiority complex on the one hand, and real narrow race-
> prejudice on the other. (152)

Montour wrote against this curriculum. His final chapter of *Brown Tom* features the plans of Brown Tom's graduating class of 1915 and includes students' intentions—not one dreamed of domestic or farm labour on their horizon. The vast majority of those who left

**FIGURE 18.** Mount Elgin, c. 1909. United Church of Canada Archives UCCA 1990_162P1167N.

Residential Schools, however, had few options besides manual and domestic labour, often for racist employers.[72] Montour was keenly aware that he was writing at a time when the horrors of Residential Schools were beginning to be more publicly discussed. But *Brown Tom* covers an era earlier than the first published fiction and memoirs on the topic, and he was at least a generation older than those writers. Montour chose to present his story not as memoir or social, political, or historical commentary, but as a deceptively simple boy's narrative with a reading level of about Grade 8—generally accessible to all, including Survivors of a system that did not teach any higher grade.

As a historian interested in *Brown Tom* as a source, I take Montour's use of pseudonyms as an important reminder of his authority as a storyteller and of the responsibility to search for meaning and lessons even in material I might consider fictional. While some readers at the time may have recognized themselves or their family in *Brown Tom*'s characters, it is difficult now to identify their real-life counterparts. Enos, of course, is the Ojibway boy from upriver, Brown Tom Hemlock. Big Brother Henry was perhaps based on Enos's brother Ralph, who attended Mount Elgin with Enos and, after leaving the school, served in the First World War as a runner, earning the Military Medal for bravery. Available Mount Elgin records from this era are sparse, and admissions and discharge forms are not to be found. Florence Wawanesa, the "Mohawk girl" with the "halting accent," is perhaps named after Montour's second wife, Florence. Other characters bear names that are common to local First Nations, including Greenleaf, Goodleaf, Hemlock, Half-Moon, Ninham, Fishcarrier, Muskrat, Roundsky, Brosette, Gibson, and Rice. Names may also have had special reference to literary, biblical, and other histories. Montour's knowledge of names and history and the obvious pleasure he got as a writer in finding names is shown in a letter to Elizabeth Graham that begins: "Dear Editor Beth G, By the way the 'Beth' part of your name means 'House' in Hebrew . . . From that you get 'Bethlehem' 'House of Bread' (Bit of useless info)."[73] Brown Tom's own last name, Hemlock, connotes a "hardy plant capable of living in a variety of environments" that is "widely naturalized in locations outside its native range."[74]

Some characters, however, carry their real names. The Principal, Reverend Mr. McVitty, for one, also nicknamed Big Mac and Mr. Mack, took over Mount Elgin in 1909 and stayed on until 1933, making him one of the longest-serving principals at the school. I only know McVitty from his correspondence with the federal government requesting funds and resources, reporting runaways, and approving new admissions and discharges of students. Montour captures him as an Irish man with "awfully blue eyes" and two nicknames, as a reverend and stern overseer "spraying" gazes over charges in church and as a fearsome disciplinarian who asked disobedient students to "remain," but who also became flustered and distraught when things got out of control. Montour and other ex-pupils describe principals from a vantage point that is distinct and critically important: while historians can ponder their correspondence with impunity and the confidence of never having been personally frightened by them, students always tell school stories from that subject position.

Senior Teacher and "Hot Gospeller" J.R. Littleproud was also a real person. John Kapayo, the Mohawk from Quebec and "Mr. Fix-it" who was an "Old Boy" of the school, was a real person. Norman Waubouse, the Carpenter and "Abenaki from Gat Valley," seems too detailed a backstory to be completely fictional, though I have not been able to confirm his identity. In a letter to Graham, Montour explained, "Re names—yes I planned on naming names, with a Boys eye view. We gave them nicknames and saw them, warts and all. Johnny Kapayo's cud was McDonald's chewing tobacco. I'll tell how we saw our leaders."[75] He added later, "Yes, I plan on a breezy, readable account of Mt Elgin and Staff as we saw it."

Montour's rationale for choosing a pseudonym or using real names is unclear. "Uncle Joe" may have been named after his father's real-life brother, Josiah, but the brother who accompanied Montour at Mount Elgin was not "Henry," it was Ralph. *The Feathered U.E.L.'s*, which he discussed as a work of non-fiction, also used pseudonyms. It is possible that this gave Montour confidence and licence to blur particulars of individuals into a single character, allowing him more freedom to craft truth from reality. It is, after all, a semi-fictional work. Additionally, perhaps he cared about getting permission but

**FIGURE 19.** Methodist Reverend and Principal S.R. McVitty, "The tall Principal with the awfully blue eyes" (107). The Rev. S.R. McVitty, "Mount Elgin Indian Residential School," *Missionary Bulletin* 16, no. 2 (April–June 1920): 160.

had lost touch with his schoolmates or found they did not see Mount Elgin the same way.[76] It may also have protected individuals from being identified in a story that came from Montour's point of view; certainly, anonymity has been used in some Residential School testimonies to protect individual privacy.

One clue to Montour's use of pseudonyms is buried in correspondence with Reverend Elgie Joblin. In his early published chapters, Montour did not refer to Mount Elgin by name, rather as "the Residential School," "a Church Home," the "Institution," and, of course, the "Mush Hole." When pulling the book together in the 1970s, however, he wanted to give the school a pseudonym that connected it to then-still-living former principals. Montour first decided on "Mount Joblin," after Elgie Joblin. Montour asked Joblin to read the manuscript and then asked for permission to use his name for the school, but Joblin declined, reminding Montour that he had been "instrumental in replacing the residential school with a day school system." He advised that Montour consider calling the school after Mr. McVitty and Reverend Oliver B. Strapp who served the school for many years. "Even so," Joblin continued, "I am inclined to think that the present mood of Indian people toward the residential schools and the part that non-Indian people had in them, would be inclined to resent this close tie with the school. If you wish to recognize the contribution of some staff member(s) it could be worked in in a less obtrusive way." Even so, Montour seriously considered "Mount Oliver," at least as late as fall 1974.[77] That Montour conflated Strapp—a decidedly unliked principal—with Joblin—who was well-liked—and Mount Elgin suggests that there are some larger threads of history at work in all of Montour's writing.

The animals in *Brown Tom* were also real, including work horses and stocks of cattle, chickens, and pigs. To Brown Tom Hemlock, the pigpen was a special source of "friendly warmth" (111) and "retreat" (111), where he could get away from it all, forget his "tumbled world" (112), and be alone, apart from an environment where students ate, slept, worked, and went to class en masse. At the same time, he was not lonely at the pigpen; the pigs were "white-haired friends" (109) he could tell his troubles to. The sty's significance is evident on the book cover (of both the first edition and this one). The drawing by Audrey Teather conveys both trouble and refuge, loneliness and friendship for a boy at an institution that was at once a school, a church, a boarding home, and a working farm that occupied the time, labour, and psyche of First Nations children.

Montour's depictions of the environment of the school in the early twentieth century are powerful. He seems to revel in writing about the natural environment around the school, using precise and accurate detail, much of which also suggests symbolic weight that might reward further study by a literary scholar. He also tends to capitalize common nouns for the school's physical buildings, like the Main Building and the Barn, as well as the Institute itself, reflecting the authority they represented and suggesting that they were due particular recognition in the view of a boy who was a student at Mount Elgin. Attuned to the everyday experiences at the school, like health and illness, as well as extraordinary ones, like a terrible barn fire, Montour ably captures the living conditions and material culture of the school.

In *Brown Tom*, Montour writes with care and beauty about his southern Ontario home and about Tom's efforts to find his place at Mount Elgin. In doing so, he animates the non-human world at a particular place and time—the animals, plants, land, and water that carried Brown Tom and Enos Montour, and many others, through life at the school. His Mount Elgin is set firmly in the living natural world of the Thames River area of southwestern Ontario, located in the Carolinian zone, a forested ecoregion located along the Atlantic coast in the United States and inland from around Sarnia, Ontario, up to Toronto. This region has a mild climate and wetlands that foster a unique natural biodiversity that includes large leafy forests and a wide range of birds and amphibians. The soil is fertile, and with a long summer climate the area has highly productive farmland. Most of the old, beautiful forests were removed for logging, farming, and industrial development, but some of them are still preserved in the First Nations reserves of the area.

Summer in this part of the world tends to be warm, humid, and verdant, alive with sounds of insects, birds, and water. And this is how Enos Montour brings us into the story, beginning with life, land, and movement:

> On a warm June evening during the First War, the Muskegan [Thames] River[78] flowed smoothly on its way to the Great

**FIGURE 20.** View of the Thames River with (likely) flat-bottomed boat in the foreground and Mount Elgin cattle and the institute in the background, c. 1909. United Church of Canada Archives, 1990.162P/1171.

Lakes. Its brown waters were littered with wisps of hay interspersed with flower petals. Haying was in progress on the rich lands that lined its banks. . . .

Along the river banks, in the deep grass, cows stood, idly chewing their cuds after a day of luscious feeding. Their eyes were closed, as if re-living the day's perfection. . . .

It was a scene of idyllic contentment.

On the bosom of that slow-moving river, in those "horse 'n' buggy days," floated a flat-bottomed rowboat. (73)

The river, fields, plants, and animals surround Brown Tom throughout the book, providing escape from and ubiquitous contrast to the built campus of the school, as well as a connection to home. The Muskegan River[79]—itself given an Anishinaabe name, replacing its decidedly English designation as the Thames— conveys Tom and Henry to the school (likely from the Muncey train station) and takes Tom and his friend Angus out for "Feasts." In the summer it is a resource for swimming and catching fish (including to sell to the school for cash to spend on "Feasts"). In other seasons, the river's "mighty waters" annually freeze, flood, and irrigate the school farm. Montour's attention to these details brings alive the beauty and experience of the natural world around the school—the maple, elm, pine, walnut, and apple trees that surround the grounds, and the vines that link and cover their trunks and crowd the pathways through the bush. We come to know the mullets, suckers, catfish, eels, turtles, and frogs that live in and around the river; the bob 'o' links, yellow canaries, hummingbirds, and insects that share the air; and the grass, wildflowers, and berries that paint the children's world around the institution. Starting the book near the chronological end of the story, Montour introduces old friends Brown Tom and Angus Greenleaf (their names echoing the muddy brown river and the green foliage that lined it) drifting in a boat on a river that still links some Ontario First Nations. The boys are nearly done their time as "inmates" and are looking back on the landscape they love. It is noteworthy that this experience of the outdoor world may have been a privilege of boys alone; the girls, Tom states, in contrast lived "quite a shut-in life" (139). It is not until a little later that we become more thoroughly introduced to the built material culture of the school, and Montour never lets it eclipse the natural world in and around it. For him, and for Tom, nature is not separate from other elements of the modern material world; rather, Tom maintains the uses, refuges, and gifts of his Indigenous world.

The built environment is also an important feature of material life for Brown Tom at Mount Elgin. It includes the playground and

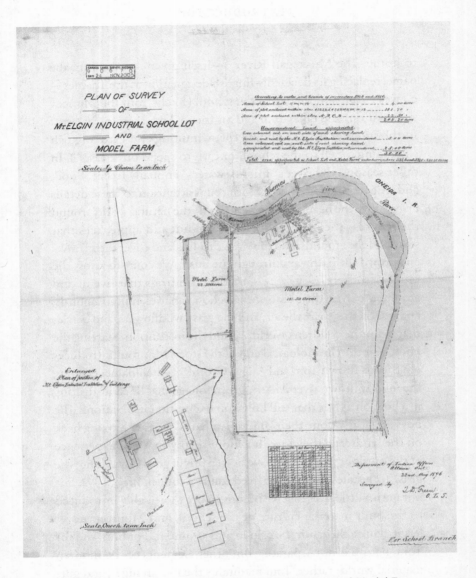

**FIGURE 21.** Map of Mount Elgin Industrial School Lot and Model Farm, 1896, showing a little of where these buildings stood when Montour attended. Map by Canada Lands Surveys, Plan Number 90670 CLSR ON, 1896.

playroom ("atop forty-five sloping steps"), the carriage shed, the white-washed pigpen, the "Main Tower," the "Great Barns," the tool shed, the corncrib, and the water pump for the tank in the attic of the main building. Nearby towns and villages mentioned in the book (Southwold, Fingal, Mt. Brydges) are likewise tied to real physical spaces. Montour does not spend a lot of time describing the interior of the buildings, especially compared with his rich descriptions of homes "on the Reserve," as Montour would say (88–90). This material world of Mount Elgin was an "object lesson" for the students, meaning that it taught the students particular lessons in order, hierarchy, inferiority, and uniformity.[80] Enos Montour pushes against these object lessons that were little able to make Tom forget home.

Clothing is another material aspect of institution life that Montour attends to in *Brown Tom*, taking on a martial tone as he describes, for example, the "numbered stockings" (110) that would have borne students' identification numbers and may well have been made or mended by girls at the institution. In January, the school "issues" toques, "usually bought in job lots from slightly damaged city fire-sales goods" (111). Both Tom's "red, woollen toque" and his Sunday outfit of a "grey suit with knee pants" smell of woodsmoke (132). These clothes are not made specifically for them but obtained a cut rate after industrial fires made them unsalable on the regular market. The boys also wear "blue smocks" (99) and "blue overalls, dotted with white" (74), with "much-laundered shirt[s] of blue" (74). Though difficult to tell from historical photographs, this was very likely true of the real Mount Elgin as well.

Of Montour's descriptions of the material world of Mount Elgin, food is perhaps the most prominent. *Brown Tom's Schooldays* begins with Brown Tom and Angus Greenleaf supping on "Loaf 'n' Lard" procured from a shop upstream from the school. With pennies senior students could earn from planting onions or selling fish to the school, they had purchased a loaf of bread and a slab of lard,

FIGURE 22. Children gathering the grain sheaves at Mount Elgin Residential School, c. 1909. United Church of Canada Archives 1990_162P1156N.

hopped in their boat, and enjoyed their "Feast" on their way back to the school. Montour's attention to the pleasures of even such a basic meal highlights the bland and barely sufficient everyday diet at the school. In the book, the word "mush" appears no fewer than twelve times: seven times in the phrase "Mush 'n' Milk" and five in the phrase "Mush Hole." Both phrases refer to the porridge served daily to students at Mount Elgin. "Mush Hole" was a nickname used by Survivors and their descendants for both the Mohawk Institute and Mount Elgin, not just because "mush" was a tiresome staple but also because unappetizing food was part of an environment of deprivation, including malnutrition, abuse, and humiliation, that was more like a miserable hellhole. The expression "mush hole" remains a shorthand for Residential Schools' deprivation and abuse.

*Brown Tom*'s opening scene also shows how students supplemented their meagre diet in a variety of ways. Food could be bartered at the school—in this case, future "Sunday Cakes" for a "right now" slice of bread (104). Other foods mentioned in *Brown Tom* did not require bartering, like raw turnips, apples, and walnuts. These foods would have been relatively easy to procure, if clandestinely, at the institution from either the kitchen stores or the garden and grounds, and Montour's granddaughters, Mary and Margaret, highlight his food memories of turnip in their Afterword to this edition. The feeling of hunger runs through the book, with the word "hungry" appearing fourteen times and "hunger" twice. Hunger is often described by Montour as a state specific to age and gender: older boys. At the time, boys' hunger may have been more acceptable (at least to discuss) than girls' hunger. Hunger at Mount Elgin is set in contrast to memories of food from home—in particular, the "gundgeon"[81] (pan bread made from sour milk, soda, and flour), pork, dried apples, and boiled potatoes—and to the boys' "dream world of full tummies" (103). Food, or "Grub," was eaten off "chipped porcelain 'dinnerware'" (103) in a dining room at "appointed tables" (103), at appointed times signalled by bells and after a long wait lined up in the "Supper march" (92).

*Brown Tom* also documents a First Nations student's perspective of two real-life events, one local and the other international: the Mount Elgin barn fire of 1915, and the First World War. In the chapter on the war, the students do "not [know] what it all meant"(144), though the war reaches Mount Elgin through "letters from home" bringing news of older brothers and dads "joining up," "donning khaki," and "doing their bit" (144). Men from Thames River communities joined other First Nations men, who enlisted at higher rates than did non-Indigenous Canadians. Many found that the uniform, at least while they were overseas, afforded them increased opportunities that had been closed to them otherwise. When First Nations soldiers returned after the war, they returned to an unequal society that segregated and marginalized Indigenous people. They did not receive benefits available to other veterans, and those who lived on the reserve after the war lost their right to vote in federal elections, which had been extended to overseas First Nations servicemen and servicewomen during the war.[82]

The war also entered their school's classrooms in history lessons, where students learned "where the 'red BRITISH line' was"; it entered "Evening Prayers"; and it became part of the soundscape of the school as war songs like "Pack Up Your Troubles" played on the "scratchy old gramophone" after prayers (145). Union Jacks were displayed in the Prayer Room and offices; missionaries even appeared in military uniform. Montour writes, I believe, about my First Nation (Munsee), my Uncle Arnold Logan, and his father, Chief Scobie Logan: "But it was when one of their own kind was reported joining the army that the War became a personal thing. The son of a famous Chief from a nearby Reserve was among the first to join up. Later they heard about recent Mt. Elgin graduates who had joined up" (145).

Montour wrote about both the Six Nations servicemen who served in the First World War and the First Nations home front in *The Feathered U.E.L.'s*: "The Indian Reserve life during those four years of War, was very much like that of other Ontario areas. In fact, the reserve and the nearby town drew perceptibly closer together, as comrade Loyalists should." Montour described how official telegrams were delivered by motorcycle on the reserve during the war and that in 1917, the Brantford and Hamilton papers were "full of casualty lists." He also explained that during the war there were some "fringe benefits": Separation Allowance and an increased demand for hay, which meant employment. All told, however, returned men "did not find their post-war homes a place for heroes to live in, but adjusted to the ways of peace and tried to forget the blood and horrors of modern war."[83]

The barn fire described in Chapter 9 of *Brown Tom* was also true to life. Fires were common in Indian Residential School history. In its chapter on fires, the report of the Truth and Reconciliation Commission reveals that no fewer than thirty-seven Residential Schools were destroyed by fire between 1867 and 1939. There were also at least forty-eight fires in outbuildings like barns. Fires were the result of shoddy construction, unsafe conditions of furnaces and pipes, dangerous equipment, and deliberate acts of resistance by students with the intention to damage the school.[84]

The 1915 fire at Mount Elgin was fearsome and destructive, killing livestock and incinerating hay and feed, not to mention razing an enormous shelter for both. The fire made news at least as far away as Brandon, Manitoba, where it was reported that the "fire totally destroyed the barns and contents of the Mount Elgin Institute" and was caused by "fire-crackers which an Indian lad fired off near the barns. The loss is $20,000, partly covered by insurance."[85] This fire is recorded in the written archive of Mount Elgin in the reports and letters of the principal. In *Brown Tom*, however, Montour accounts for the way this kind of traumatic event burns its way into memory:

> Perchance in later years, when the Mt. Elgin Grads had grown
> to take their place as men and women with the race, they
> would meet again. Perhaps as fruit pickers near Jordan's Big
> Valley; or as Comrades-in-arms somewhere in France; better
> still it could be at a Revival Service, featuring the Manass

Family Singers. They would rehash the old days in the Mt. Elgin "Mush-Hole," as they love to call it. But they would always come up with a PICTURE indelibly etched on their Memories. It was that Sunday afternoon, during World War I, when the Institution Barns went up in smoke. (124)

Montour's book gives fulsome descriptions of hunger and homesickness but is more reticent about other unsightly and serious maladies that were common at the school at the time. For example, he writes, "They were for the most part a healthy-looking group, though some of the smaller lads suffered from skin diseases and 'chapped' hands" (likely scabies, lice, or eczema) (93). Later he reports lice using the only Delaware word in the book, weelpeesh (105), and then only as a metaphor. In reality, Mount Elgin and other Indian Residential Schools were rife with lice, scabies, and other vermin that thrive and spread easily in communal settings. In the book, Tom accounts for these vermin as a witness, not a sufferer. Likewise, his telling of the story of Noah, a boy who dies of tuberculosis at Mount Elgin, is distant but still poignant.

Noah's death stands for others at the institution and documents a common pattern: first, Noah grew "unusually quiet and listless" (142), and when he finally reported sick, the doctor was called. As observed by Tom, Noah's "creeping, insidious disease came over him," and he "began to lose interest in all boyish activity" even while "chums tried to interest him in their games and outings" (143). Montour writes, "He coughed frequently and his energy was sapped away. . . . Soon after this Noah was taken away from the Institution quietly, and emptiness remained where the gentle boy had lived with his pals" (143). It is not clear in the text if Noah was "taken away" home or to a hospital, or if he had died; however, the chapter title—"Happy Hunting Ground for Noah"—tells us it is the latter. *Sites of Truth, Sites of Conscience*, the historical report of the Independent Special

Interlocutor for Missing Children and Unmarked Graves and Burial Sites associated with Indian Residential Schools, is helpful in interpreting this brief and reticent discussion of Noah's death. The report uses the term of "ungrievability" to understand widespread apathy and indifference towards deaths and burials of students. Expressions of grief about student deaths were denied in the Indian Residential School system through the failure to communicate information about deaths situations either to students or to families.[86] This dehumanization was vehemently resisted. Outside the purview of the students, in Mount Elgin's written record, there are many complaints lodged by parents and band councils about the impacts of poor nutrition, contagious disease, and overwork, as well as inadequate medical care and overall neglect faced by children. Outside the purview of students, in Mount Elgin's written record, there are indeed many complaints lodged by parents and band councils about the impacts of poor nutrition, contagious disease, and overwork, as well as inadequate medical care and overall neglect faced by children at Mount Elgin.

One of the phrases Montour uses to describe the students is the "milling herd" (92), which I believe describes the students as a unit or a group who moved around together in a seemingly disorderly way. One might associate "herd" with cattle or other animals, but perhaps Montour was thinking of the group as more holistic and connected. With "milling," it may also suggest the failed effort of the school to discipline and assimilate a group of people who remained diverse and divergent. Montour is alert to the range of backgrounds, experiences, and stages of life of the students who came to the school. He refers explicitly to Oneidas, Chippewas, and Mohawks, but also attends to diversity in other ways. There were "Seniors," who had more freedom and privilege than younger students who had not become so accustomed to the homesickness, drudgery, anonymity, and "rough knocks." There were "dandies," who cared greatly for their appearance, as well as kids of steelworkers who could tell Brown Tom about life in the great cities where their parents had worked. There were kids with no parents, "waifs and strays, orphaned children, sent here for shelter [. . . whose] lot was made harder due to the lack of those softening influences that letters from home and a little spending money from time to time can bring" (95).

Montour depicts the political and cultural differences among the students and which they would have to face when they left the institution, and this is especially clear in his depiction of the "Three Worlds" that Brown Tom encounters: the first, the "world of the home Reserve" that was "warm, secure, and not too sanitary" (86); the second, the "White man's world," "strange and challenging" where "they seemed always in a hurry" (86); and the third world of the "Institution," "neither Indian nor White. It was half 'n' half—like milk and water," a "strange admixture of the two . . . sanitary, disciplined and well-ordered" (87–91). That he describes these not simply as physical locations but as lived experiences tells us that Montour is depicting three distinct philosophies and ways of living; there is no neutral middle ground, making change and growth (for Tom and likewise Montour) more severe and violent.

Early in the book Montour describes Tom's "first world" in terms of generosity, sociability, and comfort, including visiting with and hosting Indigenous people who are from other places. Tom's first world, Montour writes, was "the world of Indian hospitality. It was a world a bit like Lotus-land, where no-one hurried or worried. Pan bread and pork gravy were always set out for the stranger, regardless of his name or tribe, so long as he came in peace" (90). Brown Tom enjoyed listening to the talk of his elders: "It was as though they had said 'I am going to work—but I don't mind being disturbed'" (91). "This was the life," he stated. "No worry, no taxes. Just enough work to keep going. The Why and the Whence and the Wherefore of Life could be threshed out to one's heart's content" (91). But on his first evening at Mount Elgin, Tom already "vaguely realized" that the institution, what he calls the "third world," was "uncomfortably efficient and put his romantic soul in the straitjacket of the daily grind" (87). Here, people were "trying to make White men out of the Indians," making his "body toe the mark" and his "mind grapple with their education" (87). This made Tom "feel insecure and unhappy" (87). He resolved that his "Indian soul would go on dreaming," as in the first world (87).

Eventually all schoolchildren who survived Mount Elgin would need to step out of the third world and into either the first or the second. This metaphor is a stark observation about the policy of assimilation as experienced by First Nations people in twentieth-century Canada and a literary device deserving of consideration: Montour is not writing history here, but he is illuminating the lived experience of Canada's Indian policy from the point of view of a schoolboy. He is demonstrating how children become conscious of racism, the blunt exclusion of Indigenous rights and souls from everyday reality in Canada. It would be up to the students to take on this battle and seek opportunity in the limited spaces available to them. At the end of the book, when fellow students discuss their futures, Mitchell Noash chides his friend Angus, whose "one great ambition in life" is to "get me one good square meal." Says Mitchell: "We must be serious. This may be the last chance we'll have to be together and there's a lot to discuss. Our people are in bondage to the White man, and their Rights are denied them. We who have some education ought to help them. They ought to get back the land, money and rights that have been stolen from them" (148). Later in the conversation, he makes reference to what is likely the 1784 Haldimand Treaty: "I know a Reserve where, by a Treaty, they were promised all the land along a river from its source to its mouth. Today they are huddled in a mere fraction of that" (149). This treaty guaranteed to the Six Nations 950,000 acres called the Haldimand Tract, located on both sides of the Grand River in southwestern Ontario.

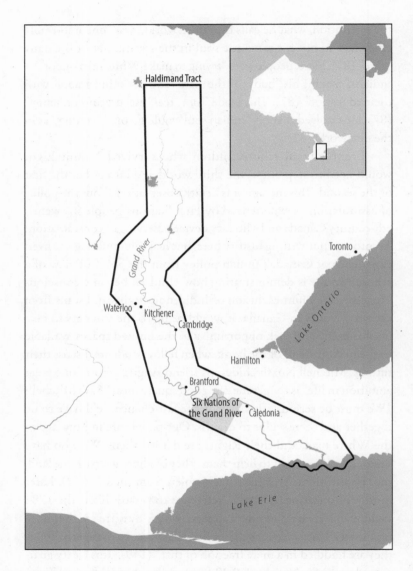

**FIGURE 23.** Map of the Haldimand Tract. Map by Julie Witmer. Base data © MapTiler © OpenStreetMap contributors.

Only approximately 48,000 acres of the Tract are now acknowledged by the Government of Canada as Six Nations territory, and the Tract today remains contested territory that is the subject of unsettled land claims, demonstrations of resistance, and a lawsuit.[87] Figure 23 features a map of the original tract and the current reserve.

Besides Mitchell and his political aspirations, other classmates dream of having their own farm, of teaching, carpentry, nursing, and further study—dreams only they may have confidence they can achieve. Principal McVitty himself seems doubtful in his words to the class: "I have tried to develop in each of you a sound mind within a sound body. Wherever your lot is cast, that will stand you in good stead" (152). In reality, the school did not provide the tools needed for success and prosperity, and students' choices were circumscribed by racist attitudes of employers that would limit their opportunities and by government policy that could involuntarily enfranchise First Nations people who had pursued higher education and professional careers, forcing them to give up their Indian status and rights.

The experience and legacy of a Mount Elgin education had an impact on the lives of all the graduates, and it has also been in many ways imprinted on the lives of their descendants. Recent efforts to commemorate and memorialize the school and the students who went there are many, and they reflect the sense of dispossession and violence that was characteristic of Indian education at Mount Elgin and beyond. In Figure 25, Enos Montour's name is featured among the hundreds of other names on a large monument at Chippewas of the Thames First Nation, located at the site of the school. *Brown Tom's Schooldays* is another monument to the school, its pages a space where readers can reflect on the injustice of Indian policy both past and present; where students can be remembered as youthful, bright, and energetic; and where the lived reality of settler colonialism that has constrained choices, dreams, and ideas is laid bare. My hope for this new edition is that readers gain access to a

HILDA MISKOKOMON
JOYCE MISKOKOMON
PETER MISKOKOMON
VENA (MONAGUE) MISSAU
CHRISTINE MOHAWK
PEGGY MOHAWK
ALEDA MONAGUE
GEORGE MONAGUE
ENOS MONTURE
RALPH MONTURE
ISIAH MOUNTPHEASANT
FRANKLIN MURDOCK
NELSON MURDOCK
DOROTHY MURDOCK

**FIGURE 24 AND FIGURE 25.** Although his surname is misspelled, Montour is commemorated by name at the Chippewas of the Thames commemoration site and monument to Mount Elgin. Photograph courtesy of Shadia Ursula Ali.

different articulation of our history than what they are used to, and that it challenges generalizations we hold about Canadian history, Indigenous people, and Residential Schools and reveals how years of everyday violence enacted by Christian missions, federal policy, and settler society have shaped the lives of all Canadians.

This edition honours the space Enos Montour created to document his experience of Canadian history and share his hope for a Canada that recognizes and appreciates the diversity, contributions, and resilience of Indigenous peoples. Montour's books did not become "standards" of Indigenous literature, nor do they fit easily within the history of Indigenous journalism or even church writing, and he struggled to get his idea for a Residential School memoir off the ground. Apart from demands of family, which were also faced by Montour, I did not have such a hard time getting *Brown Tom* off the ground this time around. I am thankful for the contemporary commitments made by Canadian publishers to bring the work of Indigenous writers and scholars into the fabric of contemporary Canadian culture and that I am alive to witness it. I am also grateful to editor Jill McConkey, who answers my communications with a resounding "yes" and follows up with me to ask, "Where's the manuscript?" I am grateful to Enos Montour's family for their support and help with this project, and especially to Dr. Elizabeth Graham for ensuring that *Brown Tom's Schooldays* could come into my hands and yours.[88]

# Preface to Original Edition

*Elizabeth Graham*

Enos Montour was born on July 18th, 1899, near Hagersville, Ontario, on the Delaware Line. His family were Delaware Indians and lived on the Six Nations Reserve. He seemed destined to become a minister. He tells us how at the age of nine he went to school and the teacher, after giving him a short verbal test, said: "That boy's going to be a Preacher, I can tell by the way he swings his arms around."

At the age of eleven Enos found himself at Mt. Elgin Industrial Institute on the Muncey Reserve, and it was here during the next four years, that he developed his love of scholarship. But after graduating with his Grade Ten diploma at the age of fifteen, he drifted for several years, getting jobs in Hamilton and Toronto. In 1919 he "ran away" from responsibility and religion and such things, and bought a train ticket out to Saskatchewan. He laughs now to recall that he landed in the most religious home in the country. He found himself going to Church with his host and he impressed the Pastor there.

In 1921 Dr. Smyth from the United Theological College in Montreal was attending a local Methodist Conference and was persuaded to call on Enos. He told Enos to save his money and go to Montreal in the fall. If he had the "Call" they would put him through College.

Enos Montour received his B.A. from McGill University in 1927, and his B.D. with first-class standing in 1929. He went back out to Saskatchewan and worked for many years among White people

in the Dust Bowl area. He was recalled to Ontario to reorganise the
mission among his own people on the Six Nations Reserve, and then
went back to Saskatchewan in 1953 where he held several appoint-
ments before his retirement in 1965.

His achievements in the Ministry both among Native and White
people were recognized with the awarding of an Honorary Doctorate
of Divinity by the United Theological College in 1975.

Dr. Montour passed away on November 18th, 1984.

This charming collection of sketches of a small boy's experiences at residential school is not intended to be autobiographical,
nor documentary, but fictional. Nevertheless, because it draws on
first-hand experience (or endurance), it provides us with an important historical vignette of an all-too-often neglected episode in our
history. Important too are the universal insights into boarding school
life that anyone who has been through it can identify with immediately—the homesickness, the close friendships, and above all, the
preoccupation with FOOD.

This is a unique story because there is so little written by the
Indians who attended these schools, and especially because it refers
to a time period more than seventy years ago—before the First World
War. Enos Montour has bent over backwards to give credit to the
good intentions of the Church, and any criticisms of the way these
intentions were carried out are understated and subtle, dealt with
humorously. The author wishes to leave history to the historians and
entertain the reader with these delightful, sometimes funny, sometimes poignant tales.

Elizabeth Graham
Waterloo, Ontario, May 1985.

# BROWN TOM'S

# SCHOOLDAYS

## by

## Enos T. Montour

Audrey Teather

# Salad Days

CHAPTER ONE

On a warm June evening during the First War, the Muskegan River flowed smoothly on its way to the Great Lakes. Its brown waters were littered with wisps of hay interspersed with flower petals. Haying was in progress on the rich lands that lined its banks.

In the air, insects of various kinds, more visible at sundown, sang their adolescent songs. The butterflies had retired for the night and it was still too early for the bothersome mosquito.

Along the river banks, in the deep grass, cows stood, idly chewing their cuds after a day of luscious feeding. Their eyes were closed, as if re-living the day's perfection. Their tails swung but slowly at the few remaining flies.

It was a scene of idyllic contentment.

On the bosom of that slow-moving river, in those "horse 'n' buggy days," floated a flat-bottomed rowboat. It was painted a bright red with the word "Institution" stencilled in white at its prow.

In that boat, two teenage Ontario Indian boys reclined gracefully. They held school books in their brown hands, cramming for the June exams, as the boat drifted down the softly gurgling current.

The lad at the prow was hunched far down, seeming almost to rest on the back of his neck, while his left foot swung over the boat's side. His smaller companion sat more erect with one hand trailing in the warm "riley" water, with his gaze ever wandering from his book.

Occasionally he put out an oar to straighten the boat's course. The sluggish river demanded little more boatsmanship than that of its scholarly occupants.

Between them was an opened paper parcel containing "Loaf" and Cheese, from which they partook in turn and munched haphazardly. Like the idyllic and sated world around them, their usually voracious appetites were almost appeased.

The smaller boy came from the south-eastern part of the Province, and was called "Brown Tom." Funny how Brown Tom got that nickname. In the library one day he came across *Tom Brown's School Days*.

"What you readin'?" asked Angus. Just to be contrary the younger lad answered: "Brown Tom's Schooldays." That became his nickname ever since. He was no browner than the other swarthy Indian lads.

It is an Indian habit to consciously or unconsciously repeat English phrases backwards. For example, an Ojibwa lady at the Meat Market said, "I wanna somma dat 'Cheese Head.'" The German farmers made very tasty Head Cheese.

Brown Tom was dressed in blue overalls, dotted with white, and a much laundered shirt of blue. He wore no hat and his hair was cut in pompadour style.

His more robust companion was a product of a central Ontario Reserve. His features were rougher, with wide cheekbones and a scar showing on the left side. He boasted of the name of Angus Greenleaf.

These boys were not "pure-blooded braves," nor were they "descended" from a long line of Indian chiefs. They were just average Ontario Indian boys, with an admixture of Anglo-Saxon blood somewhere in their ancestry. Their names adorned the Indian list of their home Reserves, otherwise they would not have been admitted to the Indian Institute.

They had forsaken the roving, forest ways of their forebears, but they had not as yet fully adopted the White man's way of life. They were neither fish nor fowl, and in themselves rested the decision as to what they should eventually become.

These boys and the boat belonged to the Mt. Elgin Indian Institution or Industrial School, whose buildings loomed in the distance and toward which they were drifting. These Schools were found throughout the country, training scholars or workmen according to the individual bent. The enrolment was entirely Indian or pseudo-Indian, and the Teaching Staff was recruited from the Anglo-Saxon world.

They were Senior boys, nearing the day of Graduation after four years within those walls. It was a happy time. In fact, they were about as ideally content on that June evening as they could ever hope to be in their so-uncertain careers.

"Funny, isn't it," suddenly exclaimed Brown Tom from his end of the boat, "how this Literature is arranged to suit the weather. Remember the time we rowed across this old river for apples in November. We were just learning in school, that afternoon:

In the stormy East wind straining

The pale yellow woods were waning

The broad stream in its banks complaining

Heavily the low sky raining.

Then, the following Easter, when it used to freeze a little every nite, so it was nice and crunchy in the morning, remember how our memory work was about:

Just before sunrise, the cold clear hours

Gleam with a promise that noon fulfils.

But Angus was neither poetic nor literary minded. Maths and Grammar were his trouble spots. His response to his companion's outburst was sarcastic.

"Yah," said Angus, "I suppose tonite we should be learning 'What's so rare as a day in June.' Well, I've got to memorize this stuff about the last of King Arthur's Knights. So keep quiet, will you? I gotta concentrate."

Brown Tom lapsed into silence after helping himself to more lunch. He couldn't help chuckling inwardly at the sheer delight of the days thru which they were passing. For, though Institution life has many hardships, there come in later life (Senior years), days that are just about perfect.

As High School students they were excused from farm work and other soiling tasks. They were the Intellectuals of the Institute and respected as such. They were hardly envied, however, by the others, who had their own cliques and interests. Even the special privileges of the Seniors did not appeal to them. These privileges were more freedom and a greater sense of camaraderie with those in charge. These were hard-earned privileges: the result of close application to their books through the years, and of having their homework done correctly and on time.

"You know," Brown Tom suddenly blurted out, "I'm not going to be like other folks when I get back to the Reserve. It's awful how ignorant some of them are. Did I ever tell you about the old man up home who could just smell gunpowder everywhere the morning after War broke out? 'My, my,' he said. 'It must be 'n awful War.' I guess he had 'n awful imagination."

Angus stirred annoyedly, and then, laying down his book, helped himself to more cheese before answering sarcastically: "Yah, I s'pose you're not gonna believe the ghost stories they tell you either. You're gonna be different. Remember that one about the fellow who ran away from a ghost that lived in the haunted house. After running steadily for about three miles, he was 'bushed' and sat down on a log. The ghost sat down beside him and said, 'Didn't we go some?' He sprang to his feet 'n' said, 'Yah, 'n' we're gonna go some more too.'"

"W-e-e-ll," Brown Tom said hesitatingly. For while he would not confess to being superstitious, yet there was a natural caution about him—especially after dark.

The shadows of the elms lining the riverbank were quite long as the boat made the last turn. The main buildings with the shining dome-like belfry loomed up on the riverbank ahead. The welcome shade would later become less welcome darkness, from which Indian boys like to be absent. To them it is often peopled with all sorts of weird and haunting creatures. They had listened to too many ghost stories in their Reserve homes to enjoy the beauty of the night hours.

"You know, Brown Tom," said Angus, "if you would keep quiet for a while a fella'd be able to get some work done round here. I'm at this Grammar now, and Oh Boy, how I hate this stuff. Let's see—Bare Subject: Judge; Bare Predicate—inferred; Object—That . . . ." Angus was finding it hard to settle down, even to Grammar. The spell of the quiet Summer evening was upon him and he too sat, watching the green banks slip noiselessly by.

For a while nothing was heard but the water lapping against the side of the boat and the occasional rustle of the Cheese wrapper.

Brown Tom was thinking of the perfection of the present days through which they were passing. They were indeed happy days. Their Senior days came after years of drudgery, rough knocks and anonymity. Now personal immaculateness, better clothing and more ready cash were their lot. They had developed at last a real appreciation of cleanliness. They even took extra baths without waiting for Saturday night to roll around.

These were indeed their "salad days." Their judgement was green and their wings were untried. They were like half-fledged birdlings even now beating their wings against the confines of the nest. They had begun to look out upon life outside these walls and were eager to be away.

The Senior boys took special pains to comb their unruly locks at Supper time. They paid particular attention to their "cowlicks" on which so much care had been bestowed through the years. No longer was their careful combing rudely interrupted with the sarcastic comments—"Tha's good nuff for HER."

Nor was the comb rudely jerked away and his soaked hair, so well and truly laid flat, tousled by a rough hand as someone said: "Gaw, he thinks he's somebody, that one." Or the more expressive Institution expression, expressive of so much bantering contempt: "Just like as if. . . ."

All that was past. Now the Senior boys possessed their own personal combs which they wiped off on their hands before replacing them in the side leg pocket of their store overalls. The younger ones, of course, could not fathom such expenditure, when such outlay would have paid for a "Feast of Loaf 'n' Lard." They, on their part, used Institution combs and these not too industriously. . . .

They respected the Seniors but left them pretty much alone. The discussions of School subjects and exam-writing trips outside left the younger ones bored and uninterested. These latter had their own concerns and they usually were to do with edibles in various forms and gathered from many sources.

The sun had set by now, and the gathering dusk made deep shadows in the hollows. The boat finally came to rest, grating on the gravel at the beach below the school. Brown Tom stepped lightly from the boat as his forebears had done from war canoes. Then he pulled the boat onto the beach, while Angus remained to weight his end down.

Then, gathering up his books and throwing the empty cheese paper out onto the current, Angus followed his companion up the steep river bank. Brown Tom, who had paused near the top, called back to him: "Did you bring the rest o' that cheese?"

"Wasn't much left," responded Angus. "I threw the paper away but I guess there's 'nuff left to trade for Sunday Cake at the second Table."

Brown Tom, who had tucked the heel of a loaf under his arm, suggested, "Better try for a couple of slices. Young Muskrat would jump at the deal. They don't get much Cake down at those tables."

"Oh, I'll get somebody to bite," said Angus.

It was quite dark when they reached the School Grounds and paused before entering the Main Building. They stood beneath the branches of a huge maple tree, with Angus leaning against the page-wire fence. Brown Tom stood a little uneasily, examining the dark pools of darkness gathering on all sides.

For the buildings were all in darkness and quiet, except for the tinkle of a piano in one of the Officer's homes. The younger children had long since retired after Evening Prayers, and the Ball Ground was possessed of an uncanny hush after the tumult of voices that had so lately subsided there.

As they stood in silence, lightning bugs (fireflies) glowed and shaded their phosphorescent light in the air about them. Over the inky black forest to the West, a crescent moon hung a deep carrot red before sinking out of sight. From the murky blackness of that forest came the nightly swishing call of the whip-poor-will. There was beauty and mystery and magic for those who regarded the darkness with calm. Our heroes were beginning to get just a little uneasy.

"You know, Angus," said Brown Tom, "I'll kinda hate to leave this old place. It's been rough but kind underneath. I think they meant well by us, don't you? But I sure hated it, that first night four years ago. I was that lonely I coulda howled to the moon."

"I guess you did howl alright when Jake Half-Moon clouted you with half a turnip," said Angus.

The whip-poor-will sounded nearer and the shadows were deepening all around them. They were both loath to admit a certain urgency to be inside with the rest of the boys.

At last Angus said: "Well, Tom, I guess the question before the House now is how're we gonna get in. I guess you better go ahead. We gotta go through the Office and explain where we've been. And I'll say this for you Tom," patting him on the shoulder, "you're a great little explainer."

They stood for a moment in silence, but their hesitation was cut short by the sudden and querulous call of a screech owl just over the fence. They both started quickly for the Office without looking back.

Tom, the great little explainer, stepped confidently in the lead.

# Brown Tom Arrives

## CHAPTER TWO

Brown Tom could never quite forget the homesickness that he experienced on the first night spent at the School. A little Chippewa Indian Boy, he had been sent to the Institution for reasons which he could not appreciate. Along with Big Brother Henry and one hundred and twenty-eight other Indian children, he found himself far from home and amid strange surroundings.

There were many cultural and educational advantages to this new life. Here one could get proper schooling and learn a trade. Homesick Brown Tom would gladly have traded all these cultural advantages for one look at his old Reserve home.

He and Brother Henry were "New Boys," a distinction that brought with it many disadvantages. They were looked upon as curios and their homesickness not sympathized with in the least. The old familiar Reserve world had disappeared and they were now surrounded by strange and not too friendly faces. Such things as electric lights, ringing bells and strict discipline intensified this unwelcome strangeness.

Older Brother Henry had always been a great bulwark in every time of distress that came upon Brown Tom. Now, however, he was not much help or comfort. He was heard to gulp audibly before answering questions. He was not feeling any too sure about things himself. This was the Big Brother who had protected Brown Tom from every danger and even worry. One day at home he had been found searching long and attentively about the house. Asked what he was looking for, he answered: "A cherry seed. Tom accidentally swallowed one and he thinks he's gonna die—I've got to swallow one too." Big, brave Brother Henry, who saw to it that Brown Tom got nothing more than glancing blows in the battle of life.

Of course, Henry would still fight his brother's battles as in that happy past. But in the sheer misery of that homesick evening, fist fights would have been mere incidents. Their whole familiar world had slid askew.

However, one last link with the former world remained. At least Brown Tom thought it did. Were not Dad and Uncle Joe still in the Office where they had parted? Tugging Henry's coat, he suggested that they leave all this and go back to their relatives.

They arrived there to discover sorrowfully that even this link was no more. The genial Principal told them kindly that their relatives had just left. Brown Tom couldn't help thinking about the Wise Men (was it?), who being warned in a dream had returned "another way."

So, they accepted the inevitable. Hand in hand they returned to the Playhouse. Here they were met with a barrage of old shoes, well mixed with odds and ends of turnip. The latter, it seems, was a sort of appetizer, to be scraped with a spoon and eaten before meals. The Chore Boys usually kept the Playhouse well supplied.

As our hero turned his back from this barrage, a direct hit occurred on the lower segment of his spinal column. It was a shoe which, travelling upward, bounded off the back of his head toward the ceiling.

This was too much. Brown Tom forthwith threw back his head and expressed all his pent-up misery in a howl to high heaven. This of course stirred the protective instincts of Brother Henry. It called for vengeance—as it had so often done in the past.

Though he did not relish the task, Brother Henry stepped forward, facing the barrage. Through the din he challenged all and sundry to a fair fight. Of course, such a challenge was met by boisterous laughter and the whole situation was saved by the ringing of the Supper Bell. This was the signal for a pell-mell surge of boys down the Playhouse steps. So ended Brown Tom's baptism of fire.

As the stream of hungry boys thinned out, one medium-sized lad stopped before Brother Henry. He smilingly pulled Henry's cap down over his eyes and in a half-serious, half-joking way said: "Gaw, the New Boy is spunky." Under this good-natured banter, Henry's anger cooled and his tightly closed fists gradually relaxed.

"You know, Boys, we lines up here for Grub," said the stranger. "Better come along."

With this, he linked his arm in that of Henry and they followed the disappearing line of boys. There began then and there a friendship between Wesley Brownleaf and Brother Henry that was to continue through the Institution years and far beyond.

Brown Tom followed behind, thoroughly miserable and unhappy. He refused to be comforted. His trouble was that he was dwelling too much in the Present. He could see no future happiness at all. The Present was all he could realize and it was too unhappily real.

How was he to know, on that first night, of the happy days that were to stretch into the future? How was he to know that these old stone buildings were to become familiar, even dear, to him?

But it was even so. From that night onward he gradually developed from a New Boy to a Regular. He went from grade to grade in school until finally he sat at the Head Table among the Big Boys. He became a privileged High School Student, staying up after the younger ones had retired. He attended parties in the homes of the Officers and made far journeys to the Great City to write off his final exams.

No longer was his nose pushed flat by the palm of a rough hand as he rounded a corner and heard a rude voice say, "Gaw. New Boy." Such disdain gave way to toleration, if not respect. Neither was he laughed at when some rude bigger boy shook him by the shoulder and demanded in one breath: "WheredidyagetyourComeFrom?" It was a favourite trick and always brought confusion and discomfiture to the New Boys.

Brown Tom's misery that night was because he dwelt too much in the present. He could not possibly foresee all these happy changes that awaited in the sunny days that lay ahead.

For there were indeed carefree days ahead for him. During the four years that he stayed there, he got to feel very much at home. The faces of the boys at the tables in the dining room became as familiar as those back home on the Reserve. He soon chose a Chum from among them, in whose company he was to find great contentment. Together they planned many an outing—fishing and hunting, digging apples preserved under the snow in the deep orchard grass, swimming and gathering walnuts in season.

As for the girls, who from across the Hall pointed out the New Boy to each other: Girls simply did not exist as yet in Brown Tom's boyish world. That world was too full of boyish interests, and that night it was too full of the misery of homesickness.

Later on, he himself came to tease and play jokes on the New Boys, who came in a steady stream yearly to the Institution. He came to pat them on the head patronizingly and say, "Never mind, Sonny. You'll get over it. Just wait till you get some of our Mush 'n' Milk."

When the New Boys left their untasted suppers on their plates, he came to take the lion's share. Their unappreciated sweets and fruits for the train journey came as a windfall to his omnivorous appetite. When the New Boys asked him what made the lights dim and go out during the Supper hour he never gave them the right answer. In his know-it-all manner he said: "Oh, it's the heat in here.

The lights can't stand it. They go out when it gets too warm." He enjoyed the perplexed, innocent comments they invariably made to this strange phenomenon.

Yes, there were to be many happy days ahead. But Brown Tom, in the poignant loneliness of that first night, could appreciate only the present.

For the time being he was thoroughly unhappy.

# Brown Tom's Three Worlds

## CHAPTER THREE

Brown Tom was a citizen of three distinct and differing worlds. In coming to the Institution that day he had passed through them all. In later years he found it hard to decide which of the three he preferred.

There was, first of all, the world of the home Reserve. This world was warm, secure and not too sanitary. It was the world of his earliest remembering. It was one whose influence was indelibly stamped on his psychic life. It would influence him through all the years.

Then there was the White man's world. It lay outside, vast, strange and challenging. He had passed through it that day and was glad that he did not have to stop. The air was a little too rarified there. He was always more comfortable and at ease when he got back to the Reserve from it. They meant well, these strange people, but they could not understand the inner life of a little Ojibwa boy. He would not try to make them understand. He would just quietly go back to the reserve. There he would be understood and appreciated. And that, without a word being said. The very air on the Reserve was different.

The third world was the present all-too-real one, the Institution. No doubt that world meant well too. But it was so uncomfortably efficient and put his romantic soul in the straitjacket of the daily grind. It was neither Indian nor white. It was half 'n' half—like Milk and water.

What were they trying to do anyway? Trying to make Whitemen out of the Indians. Well, they might make his body toe the mark and his mind grapple with their education. His Indian soul would go on dreaming as it had done on those warm April evenings on the Reserve. This third world was a strange admixture of the other two.

Brown Tom perhaps vaguely realized all this that first night. It made him feel insecure and unhappy. It made him clasp all the harder the weathered hand of his brother Henry.

Now Uncle Joe and Dad had no time for such idle speculation or analysis. Especially Uncle Joe. They had somewhere to go and they had to arrive a comfortable time before Supper. They were going to "sponge" supper and they had to time it just right. They were going back to the Reserve life after stepping out into the glare of the White man's world.

They walked away and sought shelter in a home on an adjacent Reserve. The Principal had suggested that a quick clean break would be the best for the boys. There must be no lingering good-byes, lest last-minute regret spoil the well-laid plans.

So, the one sadly, full of unexpressed emotions, the other quickly, and full of plans, they left the Office. They knew that they would find a welcome at any home they might choose to visit. This welcome would be warmer (and greasier) at one that was more of the squatter type.

Indians from other Reserves always find a welcome at these homes. More so if they know the local dialect and have conversational gifts. In the latter respect, Uncle Joe was quite accomplished. It was an old game of his to visit (or "sponge," as some rudely called it) on other Reserves. He was full of talk and stories could be told by him far into the night.

He could tell of many adventures by land and water (the latter mostly swamps and creeks, with an occasional swale). So, while Dad was "having his dark hour alone," Uncle Joe regaled the company with stories. He never really got into his stride till he held a knife and fork perpendicularly on each side of his plate.

But even before Supper was announced he was well launched upon the subject of Indian Rights. He could show all the mistakes that the British and Canadian governments had made in dealing with the Indians. He went on to show how the Indian Act could be improved.

He even offered to make a trip to Ottawa if someone would raise the expense money. He was sure he could persuade the Indian office there to make the necessary changes.

"Although," he said, "Indians are not treated very well, even there. Why, a bunch of us were there one day and we were a fine bunch too. They came from different Reserves. After dinner at the Chinese cafe we went across to a Park. With toothpicks in hand we sat down on the grass, just to kinda talk things over. We weren't doin' no harm. D'you know what? You wouldn't believe it but a great big policeman came along and ordered us to get up off the grass. Imagine that. To think we owned this doggone country—now they won't even let us sit on the grass."

This home they were visiting was built of squared logs, chinked with plaster and bits of wood. Where the chinking had fallen away, vari-coloured rags were used as a stopgap. It was a small house with a shiny black stovepipe thrust through a rusty tin "collar" on the roof.

The general-use room in which they were sitting was quite small. Light came from a coal-oil lamp on a winged table, with oilcloth cover. The walls were papered with a gaudy-coloured wallpaper, whose bulges showed that building paper formed a foundation.

Mrs. Half-Moon bustled about preparing Supper for the unexpected guests. She fried fresh pork and thickened the gravy with flour. The potatoes were boiled with their jackets on except for a strip peeled down each side. This gave the guests a start in the business of peeling before adding gravy. Then she got out the dried apple dessert and steamed the slightly stale pan bread above the boiling potatoes.

All the time she kept one ear alert to miss none of the wonderful tales. Uncle Joe saw to it that in these tales were references and tributes to the ladies. Occasionally she scolded a child who lay on the floor beside the stove, tired after an afternoon's skating on the frozen swale. He was kept awake only by the delicious odours of cooking. The close warm atmosphere produced great drowsiness.

Occasionally she deftly kicked a yellow dog out of the way. The cat's tail was harder to avoid and many were Tabby's agonized protests. Uncle Joe's stories were not at all disturbed by all this culinary display. In fact his descriptions grew more lurid as time went on. Smoke and delicious kitchen odours were a great stimulus. Even the sudden flare from grease spilled on the hot stove, dammed-up the flow only for a moment.

As the monologue went on the wife found time to pause and say: "My, My." This she did without forgetting her many irons in the fire.

Occasionally she stood with the frying pan suspended while she addressed her husband. She spoke in the native dialect and remarked that Uncle Joe's stories bore out what they had heard before.

Sometimes a question was directed to Dad, who sat in the half-light behind the huge iron stove. He sat toying with a lacrosse stick, only speaking when spoken to. His mind was with his two boys in that strange new school. How could they get along? He cleared his throat and sort of shook himself before replying. Uncle Joe hardly waited for his answer before going on with the tale.

At last Supper was ready and they were asked to pull up their chairs. Of course there were the usual protestations. These are the same the world over on such occasions. They said they really weren't very hungry. They had eaten a lunch on the train. Really Mrs. Half-Moon shouldn't have gone to all this trouble, etc. etc. To which she replied in the dialect an equivalent to "Oh, it wasn't any bother at all."

However, they would just have a cup of tea anyway. Uncle Joe's throat was dry from talking. And say, didn't Mrs. Half-Moon's pan bread look inviting all steamed through like that.

"That's what we used to call 'gundgeon bread,' when I was at the Institute," said the husband.

Then, having done justice to the amenities, they all drew up their chairs. No further coaxing was necessary. They all proceeded to put the good solid food out of sight. It was noted that Uncle Joe sampled not only Mrs. H's tea and pan bread but he made a grand circuit of the whole menu. What a blessing is a healthy appetite.

They spent the night in that hospitable home. Beds were improvised from chairs formed in an arc along each side of the stove. Their overcoats were used as pillows and rag quilts were provided to ensure warmth when the fire burned low.

The woodbox was well filled with hickory sticks and Uncle Joe told them not to worry about the fire. He would see that it kept going. In fact he even proceeded to cut shavings for morning with his tobacco-smeared jackknife.

So the house gradually settled down for the night. The smoke settled up against the ceiling, joining that of other days. The stale odour of cooking was neutralized by the frost which became more noticeable as the fire burned low.

This was the world of Indian hospitality. It was a world a bit like Lotus-land, where no-one hurried or worried. Pan bread and pork gravy were always set out for the stranger, regardless of his name or tribe, so long as he came in peace. One could visit in this way from Reserve to Reserve throughout the year. One only needed to be gifted like Uncle Joe.

Of Brown Tom's second world we need not say much. It is the world of all nations and begins just outside the Reserve. To him it was a restless, stirring and challenging world. It suggested the "endless toil and endeavour of life." It was like the city world of dust, noise and speed. Above all it was a world of taxes, doctor's bills and the ceaseless grind to make both ends meet. These were sufficient to condemn it in Indian eyes. In such a world the philosophic Indian spirit could never feel at home.

Brown Tom had often seen these people driving along the Reserve roads. In fact they sometimes appeared long before his rising time. They seemed always in a hurry, driven on by some inner urge that the Indian could not understand. They had little time to stop and "chew the fat," or to philosophize about things in general. They only stopped their horses long enough to ask the way. Then, after some kindly enquiry about Reserve health and conditions, they urged their horses on.

This was, of course, so different from the Indian way of life. Brown Tom had enjoyed the talk of his elders when their not-too-industrious work was interrupted by some chance passer-by. It was as though they had said, "I am going to work—but I don't mind being disturbed."

They would sit in the sun and talk for an hour at a time. The little boys meanwhile played with the shavings from the posts. Or perhaps they would squeeze mud-balls onto wiry whips and throw the mud into the distance.

This was the life. No worry, no taxes. Just enough work to keep going. The Why and the Whence and the Wherefore of Life could be threshed out to one's heart's content. These were their main topics.

And the third world that Brown Tom had was that of the Institution. It was neither on nor off the Reserve. It was sanitary, disciplined and well-ordered.

It was just now opening up before the two boys. Its invitation did not appeal to them very much. But for better or worse they now lived within its walls. Their names were on its Roll. They would just have to make the best of it.

Perhaps if they watched closely they might get a chance to run away one of these days.

# The Milling Herd

CHAPTER FOUR

The strangeness of Brown Tom's new world that night was aggravated by the mass of unfamiliar faces that surrounded him. Here were Indian boys of all sizes, conditions and tribes. Among them were only two familiar faces—the Turtle Boys from his home Reserve.

Brown Tom looked up and down the long line of hungry boys. The meal time lineup was the most efficient of all the day's responses to the bell. At the bottom of the line were the wee chaps pushing and complaining. Near the door stood the nonchalant Big boys, with their hair parted "just so" and their swaggering attitudes.

Brown Tom didn't know them; and in his rebellious soul, he didn't want to know them either. His one great wish just then was to get away from it all—away to the warm security of his weather-beaten home on the Reserve.

"Look away there, New Boy. We got no cakes," said a rough-looking lad halfway up the line. He had a mean expression, being especially cruel to smaller boys. Brown Tom quickly averted his gaze lest this rude stranger come nearer to enforce his commands.

The Dining-room door was suddenly opened. The Presiding Officer looked over the line and tapped the bell for the Supper march. Though it was carried out with studied orderliness, there was a wealth of smothered anticipation in that march.

Brown Tom found himself among Indians from many different Reserves. Here were the quick-moving, nervous Iroquois from
the swift waters of Quebec. There would be the big good-natured
slow-moving Ojibway from the heavy clay lands of old Ontario.
Some were quite dark and rough-featured, while others showed much
evidence of Anglo-Saxon blood. Most of them spoke English well
though the latest arrivals spoke it haltingly.

As in every human group, there were many different tempera-
ments and shades of character represented there. Here, for example,
were the dandies. They were usually among the larger lads, with
hair carefully brushed, leaving a special strand to curl just above
the right eyebrow. They were vain, touchy and asked only to be left
alone. Their popularity with the girls was something their friends
could not understand.

Others were kind and sociable, showing an interest, albeit a
condescending one, in the New Boys. They were good fellows, and
wanted their camaraderie to be recognized. They patted the homesick
little fellows and told them to run along. There were others who were
friendly but for a selfish purpose. They were friendly and interested
for the material rewards that might come to them. Especially they
looked for money or for something good to eat—things for which
the homesick New Boys would have no present appetite.

They were for the most part a healthy-looking group, though
some of the smaller lads suffered from skin diseases and "chapped"
hands. All had a healthy appetite and were keen on anticipation. Of
course the older boys were offhanded about their meals, but there is
no record of any of them leaving anything on their plates. They simply
ate more slowly and politely.

In this motley group were to be found strong dominating characters who were forever making the lives of the more retiring ones
miserable. Their influence was felt in strange and differing ways. These

bullies were very jealous and tenacious of their power. As for the timid souls, they simply submitted and by doing so, survived.

There was, for example, that morning when Table No. 4 refused to eat a bite. While the clatter of eating, utensils, and the shuffling of feet in appreciation went on all around them, they made no move to eat. They sat in stony silence with sickly grins at each other.

Here was a strange business indeed. Who had ever heard of such a thing as Indian children refusing to eat? The young lady Officer came up and urged them: "Come on Boys. Eat your breakfast."

But never a move did those ten boys make except to glance guiltily at each other. They did not dare look down at their steaming plates. The Officer in charge could not figure it out, so at Dismissal, Table No. 4 were asked to "remain"—ominous word.

After the others had filed out with sympathetic but wondering glances at the ten culprits, the whole table was asked to report to the Office. So up the Office steps they unwillingly went, pushing one of the smaller lads in the lead, and finally lined up shamefacedly before the Principal.

Now, the Principal was a great student of human nature but never had he seen anything like this. Imagine ten hungry Indian boys refusing to eat their "Mush 'n' Milk." "All right boys," said he, "explain what you mean by this. Why didn't you eat your breakfast?"

No answer came from this downcast group except the shuffling of feet and sly looks at each other.

"Well, if you have nothing to say, I have. Go back down right now, every one of you, and I'll give you one more chance to eat that breakfast. I will be down there in ten minutes. If you haven't eaten by then I will whale you with a licking that you will remember all the rest of your lives. Now go."

They went. About three minutes later they emerged from the dining-room, wiping off their chins with their coat-sleeves. The Principal smiled to himself as, from a second-storey window, he saw them saunter away toward the barns. He then turned to the programme for the day. It was a closed incident.

What had really happened was that one rude bully had been the cause of this strange misadventure. As Table No. 4 sat down, he whispered out of the corner of his mouth: "Gaw. See who starts first. He's Big Pig."

Naturally no-one craved that distinction so no-one started first. Thus was the whole table condemned because of the misdirected ambitions of one bullying character.

Their economic backgrounds were as interestingly varied as their characters. Some came from homes of the squatter type, used to living a hand-to-mouth existence, food being wherever and whenever it was found. To them the regular daily menu was a revelation, though the easy freedom of the Reserve Life never lost its appeal.

Others were the children of expert steel workers, able to command a wage of ten dollars a day. That is, for every day that they worked. And their services were in demand both in Canada and the U.S.A. Of course their weakness generally was that, having worked a few weeks, they would drift back to the Reserve just to see how things were going on there. These boys could tell Brown Tom about life in many of the great cities where they had been taken by their parents when in the mood to work.

Still others were from well-to-do farm homes and were sent here simply for the better and more continuous schooling provided. They were glad to learn better methods of farming and vowed to show their parents a thing or two when they returned home after graduation.

Others were simply waifs and strays, orphaned children, sent here for shelter. Though they shared the regular life and diet of the school, their lot was made harder due to the lack of those softening influences that letters from home, and a little spending money from time to time can bring. They looked with envy upon the more fortunate ones. But as they grew older they saw that out in the world, they could by industry and saving, provide for themselves all those things that were lacking in the present existence. After graduation they would, instead of going to the Reserve, drift into the cities where, in those days, work awaited the willing.

In the long walks that Brown Tom was later to share with these companions, he was to learn much of all this. In apple or walnut gathering for days, he was to get glimpses of their Reserve home life, a type of life that was altogether different from what his had been at home. They told him of their parents and friends, and discussed sumptuous feasts that they had enjoyed and to which they would return when this "Jail" existence was over.

All these interesting things Brown Tom was to learn later. On that first night he did not find his companions interesting at all. He did not know them, and he wanted only to be left alone. For them he was just a strange little Indian boy far from home, and he was all choked up and unhappy.

# Loaf 'n' Lard

## CHAPTER FIVE

What might have cheered Brown Tom on the first lonesome night would have been a television forecast of the "Loaf 'n' Lard" days to come. He found these to be special days, arranged personally, and not by the Institution, when the daily diet was augmented.

On these occasions a "Feast" was arranged, the ingredients of which were Bread and Lard. This Feast was eaten after, and in addition to, the regular Institution meal, usually Supper. In the Institution jargon, bread was always referred to as "Loaf"—and Loaf 'n' Lard made an ideal combination.

There was, of course, a special form of Loaf called "gundgeon" bread (probably a corruption of the word "injun"). This was a sort of pan bread made on the Reserves, from sour milk, soda, and flour. When slightly underdone, it was referred to by the more uncouth as "rib-plaster," though it was never refused by any. It was, in fact, very much in demand, but could only be secured from boys whose homes were on the Reserves adjacent to the School. Its sheer weight made sending through the mails inadvisable.

But to return to the periodic feasts. The materials for them were purchased at the nearby village store, run by an Englishman. Visits were made there, sometimes by official consent, more often without.

The kindly storekeeper welcomed this extra trade, and was generous in doling out the portions.

And the Heaven-sent money, usually a dime, was secured in different ways. Sometimes it was earned in the backbreaking work of setting out ten rows of onions at one cent a row. This work was usually done in the garden of one of the Officers' homes, after hours, when the less industrious ones were playing ball. The work, though muscle-straining and damp to the knees, was enlightened by the anticipation of the manner in which the money was to be spent.

Or again, there might come one of those special days when Dad made a lucky strike back on the Reserve, trapping muskrats. He never failed in such times to remember his boys. In fact his memory was often jogged by the letters from those boys suggesting "an enclosure in his next."

For, be it known, that the little Indian boy is as adept at writing home for money as is his White compatriot. In fact, he often has an accomplice in his homeless Chum, who is glad to assist in such composition. On the Institution paper secured at the Office, the two little Boys would grubbily inscribe their plea as they sat in the shade of the old workshop.

Anyway, the wherewithal having been secured, two little boys would disappear from the playground mob. This was usually done between Supper and Prayers. They seldom followed the main road because it was wise to keep their mission not only from officialdom, but also from the predatory larger boys. There was hardly a rustle from the dust-powdered basswood leaves as the two little figures disappeared from view along the roadside. No more was seen of them till they emerged once more near the village.

During that unseen interval, a discussion usually began as to the relative appeal of cheese or lard to go with the loaf. Butter was out of the question: one did not get enough of it for five cents. Cheese showed a little more originality, but lard usually won the day as they neared the village.

Care would have to be taken that no other boys were seated on the bench outside the store or loafing within. Having taken all precautions, they would enter quietly and in a loud whisper utter the magic words "Loaf 'n' Lard," at the same time placing the damp and grimy dime carefully on the counter. Bending down to catch these words, the merchant would understand perfectly and soon the two would re-emerge. Beneath their faded blue smocks, in danger of being squeezed beyond recognition, were the necessities for a Feast.

Again there would be just the faintest rustle among the leaves as they took to the woods. Then, seated beneath a spreading oak tree whose trunk was wreathed with luxurious growths of vines, they augmented the daily diet. It was a Feast without any fussy preliminaries. Only the breaking of the string and the tearing off of the covering paper delayed the actual eating. Neither felt called upon to urge the other to "fall to." Indeed it was not necessary.

Little was said until only the crumbs remained of the long-awaited meal. Usually, the Loaf was consumed without benefit of a knife. It was simply broken in two and it disappeared by the removal first of the soft centre. The outer crust was left to the last, and in rare cases, where it was not wholly consumed, it would be preserved as a delectable medium of Barter. In most cases, while one boy finished the remaining crumbs, the other carefully licked off the remaining evidence of Lard, still clinging to the paper wrapper.

This became another appetizing memory to be recalled in the cold dark days of Winter when dimes would become scarce. More contented now than they had been for some time, they began to notice with real alarm that the sun had almost set. Had the first Bell for Prayers rung yet? Like scared rabbits they leaped to their feet and disappeared among the foliage, homeward bound.

Now we must be careful not to convey the impression that the daily Institution Menu was not sufficient. It was Plenty, but it was not enough. What we mean to say is that, in the consuming capacity of these growing boys, there were still some vacant spaces. And Indian nature as well as Nature in general, we are told, abhors a vacuum. Hence the Augmented Diet and little boys with a peculiarly contented look, listening to Evening Prayers. Their absorption was not so much present religious appreciation but very pleasant recent memories.

Students of human nature tell us that these boys wanted more simply because the food was apportioned out to them. At home it had all been set in the middle of the table and the rule was "chacun pour soi." Had that method been followed here, it has been said, these boys would not have eaten more and they would have been content. The Institution system, however, certainly prevented waste as no-one big or small was ever known to have left anything on the plate. They were cleaned and polished to perfection.

Of course, there was occasionally the "show-off" type. He usually left his cake lying in plain view, though out of reach, on his plate. He would pretend indifference about it to the astonishment of the younger ones, but at the last possible minute, as the lines filed out after dismissal, it would disappear in one efficient sweep into his coat pocket.

Such is human nature that these Boys were always hungry. Grub was the beginning and end of all conversations. This was, of course, more true of the pre-High School years. They were not really under-nourished or ill-fed. They had simply a seemingly unlimited capacity for food—and they were quite omnivorous. What little boy is not?

And this is possibly not so strange when one considers experiments made among adults. The phenomenon occurs even among such exalted ranks as those of the clergy. At a Summer School in the pre-war days, an expert dietitian was employed to arrange the menu for a group of backwoods clergymen. These devout souls were accustomed, on their daily rounds of visitation, to meals at all times and in all places. These were invitations which they could not very well refuse. They were simply victims of their circumstances and calling, and they bore their afflictions bravely.

Well, the dietitian, who held a high Diploma from an established College, planned the meals with painful efficiency. They were scientifically exact and carefully arranged. Each individual received the proper amount of vitamins, calories and whatnot. They were served delicious omelettes, custards and a variety of salads. Of course these things were duly partaken of amid polite and lofty topics of conversation.

But there was a sense of unease among the Brethren. They were not altogether happy. There seemed to be what the poet has described as "an aching void." So as the group left the Hall, two of the Brethren reached for their black felt hats and started downtown. Where were they going? Answer: to augment the daily diet.

In the course of their leisurely walks and philosophical discussion they had discovered, quite by accident, a cosy lunch counter. Here they could secure the good old favourite victuals and they could continue eating in the manner to which they had become accustomed.

So let us not judge too harshly these furtive figures, darting in among the basswood leaves or sauntering up the land with a suspicious bulge under their blue smocks. These latter were probably sent to buy the necessaries for some larger boy. Brown Tom soon got to know all the trails and tricks. And his capacity for augmented diet grew with the years.

But on that lonesome night, he sat absorbed only in the present, unconscious of the happy adventures to come. And as he sat so disconsolately, eager tho' chapped hands were reaching out for portions of his untasted Supper. What a windfall it was to have a homesick New Boy at their table. Those who sat too remote to share the spoils were taunted with the remark: "Gaw, don't you wish?"

To all this the New Boy was utterly unconscious.

# Brown Tom Makes a Deal

CHAPTER SIX

Brown Tom found himself in a food-rationed, hungry School. Away from the untidy comfort of his Reserve home, Brown Tom found his new surroundings strange indeed. As a New Boy, he found the lining up for meals so different. Of course, they were all ravenously hungry for nourishment.

There were strange goings-on especially before Sunday Dinner, when "Sunday Cake" was served. This delicacy was doled out, generously covered with sweet sauce ("Goo" the boys called it).

What made Brown Tom wonder and shudder was the way Big Boys like Angus Minabin acted. Dropping out of the lineup, Angus, a rough lad with pockmarked face, would address some hapless little boy with threats.

"Don't you fergit now, Hilton. 'Send it,' you know." Then added ominously, "Or else." As he said this he ground his fist into the palm of his other hand.

"Uh-huh," responded the unhappy Hilton, looking down and rubbing one shoe over the other. He was an Iroquois lad with black eyes and quick, jerky ways.

Then, tossing his carefully combed bangs out of his right eye, Angus swaggered back into line.

Brown Tom and his chums, from many different Reserves, were much preoccupied with food. Or "Grub," as they called it. They eagerly anticipated each meal and their chipped porcelain "dinnerware" was licked shining clean.

They talked before and after meals about days back on the Reserve. They relived "Feasts" at the local store, when a few cents came their way. In fact they lived in a dream world of full tummies.

As the handbell was sounded, the long line of overall-clad hungry lads wound into the Dining-room. They took their places at their appointed tables, without too much pushing or disorder. A young English lady was supervising and between the rows of Boys' and Girls' tables, a "Great Gulf was fixed."

She sensed a certain tension among the tables which she could neither locate nor understand. She was much intrigued by these peculiar undercurrents. In fact, these native children had strange, subtle understandings and jokes entirely foreign to those in charge. Sometimes a ripple of laughter or excitement would break out at one table.

However, by the time the Officer had arrived there, all was serene. Everyone was eating with all too evident relish.

Brown Tom, a chubby lad with light brown complexion and cheerful ways, soon learned School habits. He found what the mysterious and threatening message to the unhappy Hilton meant. As soon as the meal got under way, Grapevine messages began to pass from table to table. They got through in spite of the greatest watchfulness of the Supervisor. Of, course, it was very difficult for one Officer to watch so large a group. Often the message reminding Hilton to "Send It," was passed to some boy directly under the Officer's gaze. In that case, he went on eating his beans as tho' he had not heard.

But, as soon as her attention was directed elsewhere, he would give the boy in the next row back of him a fearful dig in the ribs. Then, in a hoarse stage whisper, he repeated the message: "Tell Hilton to 'Send It.'" Poor Hilton.

To his amazement Brown Tom saw Hilton's "Sunday Cake" being passed up the line to the waiting Angus. Then he realized that Hilton was paying a debt of honour. He had agreed to exchange it for a piece of Loaf 'n' Lard, away back last Wednesday. Hilton was "Paying for a Dead Horse."

Brown Tom recalled how last Wednesday, Angus had boasted of going on a "Feast." To the admiring smaller boys he taunted: "Don't you WISH?"

Having received a few dimes from home, Angus withdrew one from the Office. Then, he went on a splurge at the small country store.

Five cents, in those happy days before the First Great War, bought a fresh loaf of bread, and a second five a fair gob of lard. But Angus was wise enough to leave the heel of a Loaf, well larded, from the "Feast."

"Who'll give me 'Sunday Cake' fer this here? Speak up boys," he invited, walking around the Playroom.

It usually happened that some little boy succumbed to the Great Temptation. Having just come in from the Mid-winter cold, anything edible had a great appeal.

Little Indian Esaus that they were, they were forever selling their Food-Right for a mess of pottage. The "Thursday cookies" were bartered for a juicy apple in mid-afternoon, or for bits of Candy, with accretions, from overall pockets.

Some even Bartered away their morning "Mush 'n' Milk" to satisfy "Coffee-break" hunger. Of course Bartering dates back to the Morning of Time and reached its heights with beaver pelts at the Hudson's Bay post.

Naturally the Officers frowned upon the whole Barter system. It upset the nutritional balance that they had so carefully set up. Each child had been allotted the bare minimum necessary to carry on.

There was to come a Dark Sunday when even Brown Tom was ordered to "Send It." But this Sunday was Hilton's fateful day of Payment. Seeing there was no way out, and knowing the Penalty for refusal, he decided to pay up.

Thus, the unhappy Hilton's "Sunday Cake" started on its long journey to his Creditor. Of course Hilton's thumb was well plastered with sauce before letting go.

It passed down the line from hand to hand, following the same course that the message had taken. But did it arrive "in toto"? That would be too much to expect of humans of any race. In fact, the passers might well have said "Excuse the Thumb," for that digit played an important part in the transit. Those thumbs were licked off with relish as the rim of the saucer was let go.

With halts, followed by quick jerky passes, the "Sunday Cake" would finally arrive. Just about then, the bell would ring for Dismissal. But there was not a soul dismayed.

The cake, now denuded of all Sauce, was quietly shoved under the bib of Angus's overalls. Then that worthy walked nonchalantly from the room.

Later, while basking in the sun, Angus patted his stomach and boasted to Welby Half-Moon, "Welby, you could crack a weelpeesh (louse) on my tummy anywhere. I'm that full."

"Gee, you're mean to those little fellas. It makes them feel so bad," scolded Welby. "You know you 'n' me's gonna have an awful fight over that some day."

"Don't fight me now, Welby," suggested Angus, adding: "I'm too full," before turning over to doze.

Out in the Playground, Brown Tom put his arm around the unhappy Hilton's shoulder in sympathy.

"Oh, I don't like Sunday Cake—much," gulped Hilton. Then throwing off his chum's hand, he burst into tears and ran away to the Carriage Shed.

Tracing his finger along the polished Carriage wheels, he forgot for the moment his Sunday sacrifice.

But there came a Sunday when Brown Tom's Cake saucer was missing. Florence Wawanesa and Wilma Leaf, Kitchen Girls, stood after dinner, looking at his place.

"Poor Brown Tom," said Florence. "He had to 'Send It.'"

"I bet that big ape of an Angus Minabin got it," commented Wilma. "I'd sure like to slap his big fat face. He's that mean to the little fellas."

"Would you?" teased Florence. "Angus has such nice hair, combed down over his right eye. Look at him swagger out there."

The two girls moved over to the window, watching the boys at their rough tumbling play.

"Well—maybe not too hard," relented Wilma.

Officer Fern Jackson stepped into the room and saw the two girls, with arms around each other's waists, watching the boys. She saw, understood, and quietly withdrew.

"Brown Tom isn't out there," said Florence, searching the yard.

"Oh, I bet he's down at the pigpen, telling his troubles to the pigs," explained Wilma.

Welby Half-Moon had overheard little boys from the Third Table whispering. In awed tones, Ezekiel Rice was saying: "Gaw, Brown Tom had to 'Send It.'"

Missing him from the Playground, after dinner Welby went down to the pigpen. There he found the sad but wiser Brown Tom.

He was having his "dark hour"—alone.

# Too Big for Santa Claus

## CHAPTER SEVEN

Brown Tom was homesick and unhappy. Christmas was near in the Residential School—the time of Good Cheer.

But swarthy, tousle-headed Brown Tom refused to join the Christmas fun. He remembered the untidy comfort of his Indian Reserve home. There was warmth and freedom there. Freedom to come and go; freedom "to get comfortably dirty."

Back there, you ate when you got hungry and slept when you could stay awake no longer. His homesickness, however, gradually wore off. The rough-and-tumble school life he could take.

What he refused to accept was being told that Santa Claus did not come to this School.

This was a real uncushioned blow, since he had no-one to confide in. He simply could not think of a world without Santa. Somehow, somewhere, he would find the answer.

The White School Staff did not bother him too much. The tall Principal with the awfully blue eyes, nor the Vice-Principal with his "Hot Gospel" religion. As for the ladies on the Staff, they were a real comfort to Brown Tom. They looked so warm and cosy and smelled so nice when you got near them.

But the recurring thought of "Life without Santa" plagued his restless mind. Was this White man's School the one place that Santa never visited? Why?

Rough Mohawk boys laughed uproariously when he timidly asked about Santa. They tousled his hair and squashed his nose, saying: "Gaw, Brown Tom still hopes." After that, he kept his fears to himself.

Christmas day itself was so different here in this school. He missed the Concert and Tree in the old Mission Church back home. He missed also the happy visiting in the homes of his relatives.

At night, after "Lights Out," he snuggled under the blankets and told his chum Alby Lazarus of the good times back home. He went into drooling detail about all the meat and potatoes; the gravy and the Indian pan bread. While the older boys talked about Girls and sex, the younger ones talked about Food. Grub, they called it.

Christmas wasn't much in this School Home. It was just a little brighter than other days. There was a small handout of cream candies and an orange to each child.

They all sang "Hark the Herald" and there was a bit extra to their meals. The usual "Sunday Cake" was larger and with more "goo" dripping from it. The meat was cut in slightly larger portions. Still, it was nothing like Christmas back on the Reserve.

For, one important thing was missing in all this—Santa Claus. It was all very confusing to a little boy. No Santa.

Brown Tom couldn't believe or accept that. Santa must be around somewhere.

He remembered that Santa had never let him down back home. In all his eleven years Santa had never failed him.

Yes, even in Hard Times, Santa had always managed a visit. Sometimes in the New Year, he had gone breakfast-less to school. Yet, a candy cane, a licorice plug, or some simple toy showed Santa's visit.

Why should Santa disappoint his Brown Tom in his White man's School—this "Mush Hole," as the older boys called it? Oatmeal porridge had never been served so regularly back home as it was here.

Brown Tom remembered one night when he was seven. He had been very very naughty. And on Christmas Eve, of all times. He had snapped at everyone, and pouted and cried all evening.

He had been warned, too, about what might happen to nasty little boys at Christmas. Santa would only leave a switch from the Bush for him. No candies for naughty Brown Tom.

But the naughty boy would not be consoled or warned. As a final gesture of Revolt, he had hurled his shoes away under the couch. What did he care about tomorrow morning?

The shoes struck the wall and bounced back to lie hidden. They were there as evidence of his childish, tearful temper.

He remembered so well that awful Christmas morning. His brothers and sisters were exulting over Santa's gifts. Brown Tom's tears had dried and he had quite forgotten what had so upset him.

He recalled now how his shoes lay that morning—right where his naughty hands had thrown them. He was afraid to look into them.

Finally, he ventured closer. And—Wonder of Wonders. There were candies in them. He crawled out from under the sofa with a sheepish grin. Here was no switch as threatened. In his shoes were candy and an added orange.

Now, at the School Farm, Brown Tom had a secret hiding place. He went there when he was disturbed and upset.

He enjoyed getting away from it all to the whitewashed pigpen. There he stood watching his grunting, white-haired friends. Few of the other boys came here, except at pig-feeding time.

Here, miserable and upset, he could "have his dark hour alone." Good old Indian Santa, mused Brown Tom. He never let Indian boys and girls down. No, not even when they were naughty.

But Christmas had come and gone in the "Mush Hole." Santa did not show up. The White man's way of life and the rough teasing laughter of his schoolmates jarred on the soul of Brown Tom.

Of course, he did not really hang up his black numbered stockings that first Christmas Eve. He had heard enough teasing and "cracks" about boys who expected Santa.

But, after "Lights Out," Brown Tom crawled out and arranged his shoes side by side. He then carefully draped his stockings over them.

Surely these rude, loud-swearing boys were wrong about Santa. He could understand quite readily how Santa would pass them up. They were BAD.

But, surely, Santa would not neglect his Brown Tom.

However, Christmas Day dawned just like any other day. With the ringing of First Bell only a few minutes later, there was the usual din of boys stirring about. There was the wrestling and shoving of beds around. There was the odd fist fight, which was quickly quelled by the older boys. Then the "Thundering Herd" went pell-mell down the stairs to the various chores.

Brown Tom found his shoes and stockings at the foot of his bed. They were just as he had left them the night before—empty. As he lay across his bed, looking down at them, Jake Fishcarrier, a sarcastic Third-former, came along.

"Gaw, Tom is lookin' fer Sandy Claws," he teased, rumpling the younger boy's hair.

That wasn't so bad. But, when Norman Sabima, a Senior Entrance lad came along, his comment really hurt. Putting a kindly hand on Brown Tom's head, he comforted, "Tom, you're too big for Santa Claus now."

A great lump came into the young lad's throat. Tears welled up into his eyes. He didn't want to be too big for Santa Claus.

All he longed for just then was his Injun Bush home—where Santa always came. He longed for its disordered warmth and careless comfort. A bewildered, confused and homesick boy, he stood watching his gay companions returning from morning chores. They were all ready for their "Mush 'n' Milk."

But Brown Tom found his boyish world all tasteless and forlorn. And this, on Christmas Day, when all should rejoice.

Of all this, Brown Tom, Indian-like, uttered not a word. But, surrounded by sixty shouting, wrestling boys, he was as lonely as a deserted prairie shack.

Kinder boys had tried to explain that Santa did not come the same way here that he did on the Reserve. But Brown Tom never let his faith in Santa weaken.

Christmas was followed by New Year's. All this while, a great unsettled question hovered over his boyish mind. He still wondered and grieved.

Late in January, an issue of red, woollen toques was made to the boys. These were usually bought in job lots from slightly damaged city fire-sales goods.

As the kindly Vice-Principal handed Brown Tom his toque, he said, "Watch out for those candies inside."

A great upsurge of Hope sprang into the soul of Brown Tom. Here were the missing candies. Here, dear old Santa was vindicated. He had come after all, but his treats had been overlooked.

Brown Tom's hand trembled as he reached for his woollen cap. His face flushed with pleasure. A great mystery had been cleared up. A vast sigh of relief welled up from his boots to his throat.

But the teacher, noticing the lad's agitation, warned: "I don't think I'd eat those mothballs if I were you."

After that, Brown Tom stumbled from the room, heading for his pigpen retreat. The teacher stood, jangling his keys. "What a strange little boy," he mused.

At last, in the friendly warmth of the pigpen, Brown Tom was welcomed by friendly grunting. The lad couldn't help noticing what an orderly menage these pigs kept. Meditating on this, he pushed the great let-down to the back of his mind.

Here at the foot was the feeding-trough. Over there was their bed of clean straw. And away over there, in the corner, was their "Powder Room."

Strange creatures these pigs. So mused the bewildered mixed-up Indian boy. His faith had been shattered, but here, for the moment, he forgot his tumbled world.

Finally, hearing the First Bell ring for supper, Brown Tom straightened up and faced Reality. Santa had definitely bowed out of his life. He now faced and accepted the Santa-less years that stretched before him. For, in that moment, in that Farm School pigpen, Brown Tom grew up.

He WAS too big for Santa Claus.

# Brown Tom's Happy Days

## CHAPTER EIGHT

Brown Tom was supremely happy. In fact, he was gurglingly happy in his own Indian way. For, tomorrow he was leaving for a month's holiday at home. Home, on his own Reserve.

The mow, from which he was throwing down Alsike hay, was oven hot on that July evening. But there was bubble joy in the heart of the Ojibway lad—Joy such as comes seldom in a lifetime.

His older brother, Angus, had breezily arrived on the scene that afternoon. His mission was that of escort, in those "horse and buggy days."

A lad of 18 summers, he was dressed in the full glory of a "peg-top" suit of navy blue. That suit had been carefully pressed beneath the mattress on the previous night. His knob-toed, tanned shoes were well shined, and his hard sailor hat, with its vermilion band, was set at a jaunty angle.

He had been welcomed at the Office and was to be the guest of the School for the night. On the morrow, he was to conduct Brown Tom down to catch the 10:15 train.

So passed a happy night for Brown Tom, whose exulting soul even Evening Prayer could not dampen. He did not resent even having his nose playfully squashed by the palm of a Big Boy. "Gaw, Brown Tom is joyful tonight," the latter remarked.

The Ojibway lad slept with a smile on his face and, long before First Bell, was astir. He sat on the side of his bed, fully clothed, telling his chum Welby about his plans. Tho' that chum was a homeless orphan, he basked in the reflected happiness of Brown Tom.

At last train time drew near. Farewells and good wishes were said, with Brown Tom feeling tolerant toward the whole world. Even the Indian Institute, familiarly called the "Mush Hole," was included. The first strangeness and the rigid discipline were now all past.

As they sat in the day-coach, admiring the blue plush furnishings, Angus gave out pointers on behaviour. With all the worldly wisdom of 18 years, he advised: "Mustn't point at people," and "Don't open your mouth every time you look back."

Late that afternoon, they stepped off the train at the village near the Home Reserve. Here they were greeted by old familiar friends. Some of them Brown Tom found it hard to remember. "Mush 'n' Milk must agree with them," and "My, how big he is" were the usual comments.

Angus bought some overripe peaches, advising Brown Tom to "wipe off his chin after eating." Then they sauntered along the sidewalks of the little market town.

Getting a ride part way home on a hayrack, they gathered up their parcels at the store which catered to Indian credit trade. They next bought some boiling beef, baker's bread and buns to eat along the way.

The road was hot and dusty as the wagon lazily clacked its way in the afternoon sun. The white dust rising from the road powdered the milkweeds alongside. Only the deep blue of the Chicory plant showed through this powdery whiteness.

The discussion on the hayrack was mostly about the price of baled hay and the rent of pasture land. The younger lad cherished his own thoughts during the slow, hot journey.

They finally arrived at a bush trail that led a mile across to home. Gathering up their scattered parcels, they dismounted. Waving to the driver, Angus farewelled: "See you at the Garden Party."

It was cool in the deep woods. Where the sun shone through the clearing, the pungent odour of pine cones and wild strawberry plants was strong.

Coming out to another Reserve road they leaned against the rail fence, looking at their Indian home. It was only a dilapidated frame house, unpainted through the years, standing on a 50-acre lot.

But it was Home to them—the one spot in all the world most dear, in an indescribable way. Through the long, frosty nights at the Boarding School, Brown Tom had dreamed about this place. Perhaps his fancy had woven embellishments about it that were too grand for the Reality. For a moment, Brown Tom was taken aback by its rundown appearance.

It was an old draughty building with rotting sills. The door frames were slightly out of plumb by the general sag of the whole structure.

Yet, it was Home. It warmed the hearts of the two travellers with childhood memories. Brown Tom tried to convince himself that it was better than the brick and stone of the Indian Institute.

But was it? He was ashamed of the doubts that assailed him. Certainly no brownstone house in the cities that he had passed thru could mean as much to his sentimental and homesick soul.

Yet, it was just a dark old frame building back on the Reserve.

Perhaps the Scot's "wee hoose 'mang the heather" had ants in the sugar. Then too, the "Old Kentucky Home" and the "Tumble-down Shack in Athlone" were not architecturally superb. Certainly the "Old Sod Shanty on the Claim" had a garter snake or two plopping from its walls.

So, without being too critical, let us weave a sentimental song about Brown Tom's "Old frame house on the Reserve."

Tall weeds stood around the doorway and overran the chipyard. The only sign of industry or care was the recently mowed hayfield at the rear, where the renter had taken off the Timothy hay.

A half-hearted attempt at a garden showed through a stand of ragweeds. The gardener had abandoned it at the call of Berrypicking near Burlington, for it was at this work that Angus had earned the train fare for the younger lad. Brown Tom's people were of the come-and-go squatter type.

Their love of home, however humble, was because only here could they really be themselves. Among the Anglo-Saxon people they were tense and on guard. They could return here when the outside world had become too cruel and unfriendly. Here they came to people who accepted them without lengthy explanations. Here they found that response from fellow-creatures so essential to human happiness.

Brown Tom was almost deliriously happy during those first days at home. He hunted crabs in the swale and ate apples from the thorn-apple tree by the gate. His meals were few and at irregular intervals. Yet they were to him more tasty than the "Mush 'n' Milk" and other dainties of the Institution menu.

The rigid discipline and regulated life of the School were forgotten. It was nice to get comfortably dirty again.

They slept late on straw-filled ticks, supported by heavy wooden slats. He played all day, eating only when Hunger became too strong, and everything was grist that came to his digestive mill.

Sometimes he ate cold beans scraped with a wooden spoon from the bottom of an old black iron pot. Or, again, it was cold pork gravy with summits of meat protruding here and there. Sometimes they ate bread and milk from a large pan on the front steps in the moonlight.

Only one persistently recurring thought marred the bliss of Brown Tom's vacation days. This was that Time was passing. Soon these happy holidays must give place to Indian Institute days once more. He had many a "Dark hour alone" because of these unhappy reminders.

Philosophic Brown Tom wondered if there wasn't some way of making Time pass more slowly. Standing beside the crab-haunted swale, he mulled this over. Could NOW be prevented becoming THEN too soon?

It was worth a try. So he stood erect and said N-O-W, very slowly, relishing that special part of Time. But ere the echo of his voice had died away, Time had marched steadily on. So, on with the Play.

Thus, the vacation days sped by eagerly and unimpeded. Finally came the time when he was due back at the Boarding School, sometimes called "the Mush Hole," at other times the "Jail," by the boys. It was about the time that Dad shouldered his pitchfork and went forth to the Fall's threshing.

It had been nice to be home. There was much about this carefree, undisciplined life that he would miss. But now the White man's world was calling him, and he was strangely ready, almost eager.

He now looked forward to reunion with his old classmates. There would be New Boys to meet and tease, and there would be strange new subjects to study in the Entrance Class. The home folks noticed this suppressed eagerness, as he packed his old suitcase. They saw and wondered.

Their boy had been won from them to a new and different Way of Life.

# Trial by Fire

## CHAPTER NINE

Sunday, May 16th, 1915, dawned a beautiful pre-summer day. It was the second year of the First Great War. But to the native children, Loyalist though their ancestors were, that was all so far away. They had more immediate things to worry about.

Brown Tom Hemlock and Angus Greenleaf had many plans even if it was Sunday "Go to Meeting Day."

On that perfect Spring morning, even the Barefoot Boy who "called the cattle home" didn't mind the early rising and the dewy walk. His was the "sleep that wakes in laughing day." While the mists rose from the cool pasture flatlands, dotted with sturdy butternut trees, the cow-caller trudged on.

A boy's day in May could be a beautiful thing with bob 'o' links and robins swaying from the weeds, pouring out their hearts in song. Yellow canaries darted by, while hummingbirds drank from the nectar of flowers, their swiftly beating wings making an almost audible "whirr."

Welby Ninham, the Oneida cow herder, was a real "Barefoot Boy" of the school books. He had the cheek of tan, the turned-up pantaloons and the merry whistled tunes. It was too early for strawberries to redden his lips even more.

On such a perfect day it seemed nothing could go wrong in God's most perfect world. But that was the day that saw dark Tragedy strike, threatening the lives of all.

Up in the playroom atop forty-five sloping steps, Brown Tom and his faithful chum Angus Greenleaf were casually spending the late afternoon that Sunday. Angus was scraping a half turnip with the side of a spoon and enjoying eating the moist mulch. Brown Tom was practising making a half-shut jackknife open and land blade down.

Summer insects droned lazily in the afternoon sun. The rest of the sixty-five boys had scattered far afield. Some were frog hunting while others went to the Deep Bush Variety Store to "window shop."

Around 4 p.m. the huge bell in the Main Tower began to ring, slowly at first, then gaining speed like an alarm.

"Milking time," said Brown Tom, going toward the playroom door. "I wanna see those giggling girls."

"You would," exclaimed Angus, resuming his lunch scraping.

But, looking out the door Brown Tom shouted: "Oh, Gee Whiz. God help us." Angus came running and looked out horrified, as the Milking girls with clattering pails let out terrified screams.

Out from the open door of the hay mow of the Great Barns a black whirling column of smoke was rolling toward them. The dry old hay was ablaze and roofs were ready to lift off.

These large barns stood on 10-foot-high cement walls and covered a rectangle of 100 x 150 feet. They enclosed a central courtyard. In these barns were housed the Milking Centre with a huge Melotte cream separator. Horse stables covered the other part, with a large tool shed and harness room. Above it all was the tinder-dry hay all-ablaze.

From the playroom the boys saw that only an open-work corncrib with slatted sides stood between them and the dense cloud of smoke.

Clattering down those steps, Angus shouted, "Let's get outta here before that corncrib starts to burn."

The lady teachers and kitchen staff now joined the horrified girls, looking helplessly at the burning barns. The girls still clutched the shiny pails in their hands.

Then, the usually calm, dignified Clergyman—Principal Rev. S.R. McVitty, a Belfast minister—just awakened from his Sunday siesta, arrived. He usually hummed old Methodist hymns as he inspected his busy polyglot charges.

But, today, his vest was unbuttoned, his hair wind-tossed and his nerves unstrung. He stood transfixed for a moment, but as other male members of the Staff arrived, he began to issue orders right and left.

In that moment he envisioned the weeks of investigation he would have to undergo to account for all this. The Church, the Indian Department, Insurance Company and Missionary Staff would all await his answers.

Pandemonium now broke loose with shouting and the screams of imprisoned animals. The men on the School Staff quickly gathered around the dishevelled Principal, "Big Mac."

With a mighty roar the flames broke through the barn roof and shot hundreds of feet into the air. This mixture of thick black smoke and mounting red flames could now be seen for miles around.

The usually immaculate Vice-Principal and Senior Teacher J.R. Littleproud, who had the habit of tucking a small handkerchief inside his white linen collar, now came running collarless, adjusting his pince-nez glasses. He was ordered to the office, this dainty, saintly type, to phone Mt. Brydges, Southwold and Fingal, all towns encircling the holocaust. Their ancient, horse-drawn fire-fighting equipment soon drew near to the disaster area.

One of the earliest at the fiery scene was Mt. Elgin's "Old Boy," Johnny Kapayo, Mohawk Alumnus from a Quebec Reserve. He was trilingual. He was admitted at an early age as an unlearned urchin, but he later mastered a trade—Master Mechanic, a sort of "Mr. Fix-it."

When Johnny was old enough to return to Quebec, he was taken "on the strength" of the School Staff, with a gang of boys to train in handling tools. He also took unto himself a wife from among the Girl Grads. So he came, looked, and liked what he saw, and found his life work.

The usual juicy tobacco cud in Johnny's jaws was rotating wildly as he gathered a gang of older boys around him to hunt up the unused fire hose. He reported to "Big Mac" and soon located the fire hose. More hose was found in the tool shed. Water was poured on the smouldering corncrib, which was a buffer between the fierce mounting blaze and the main buildings. It was a steady contest between water and fire.

Irish Stockman Bamford, bunions and all, and Farming Instructor James Henry joined the horrified members of the School Staff.

One oft recurring thought was "how did it all start?," and what upset them more was wondering whether all the boys had been safely accounted for.

The watchers stood petrified, gazing at the fearful, devouring flames. They could not stay to watch, yet they could not walk away, held by the lurid flaming glow a few yards away.

We shall leave them there and see how the Cow-caller lad was doing with his slowly moving herd as they returned to the barns for milking time. Welby set his pace to theirs and gazed at the vari-coloured clover tops, and listened to the bird calls. A goldfinch on some personal mission hung and swayed over the sweet apple blossoms.

Suddenly Welby looked up toward the barns, just in time to see the whole roof lift off the barn, with flames mixing with the billowing smoke.

"Oh Megosh," he shouted, adding: "and Gee Whiz. Jest look at that."

The cows ambled peacefully along, totally unaware of the whole awful sight.

Then, out of the corner of his eye, the Barefoot cow-caller saw a sight that called for quick action. A powerful thoroughbred stallion had broken loose from its box stall, kicking the doors and wooden walls to splinters.

With its mane and tail ablaze, this berserk animal was heading down the lane on a collision course with the ambling cows.

"Just one thing to do," said Welby. "Get the heck out of here—and fast," as he climbed the fence and rolled into the sweet-smelling clover, scattering the feasting bees. There he lay panting, waiting for the crash of horse bone on solid cow flesh. He expected to see Beef Steak and Hamburg Meat scattered all about. He held his ears.

But nothing happened. He finally looked up and saw the cow-filled lane divided equally at the centre, giving the enraged stallion a clear trail down the lane. Away it pounded to the flats, bellowing wild screams and snorts such as man or lad had never heard before on land or sea.

The cows with heavy-laden udders moved ahead anxiously to get where girlish hands would release them of their milk. As they regrouped a fire-guard turned them back from the ravaging flames. With one voice they set up such a bawling that could be heard clear "across the sands of Dee."

Toward evening, when the Inferno had burned itself out, some sixty boys of all ages wandered back from their Sunday travels. Those who had a dime had been to see if Forest Variety store was open on Sunday. Loaf 'n' Lard tasted good on any day but they were feeling just a wee bit guilty about breaking the Sunday laws. Like the Scottish lad who dared to "whistle" on the Sabbath, they expected a severe reprimand.

The supper prepared by the kitchen staff was hasty and light. Apple sauce made from brown dried apples was usually the dessert. Of course, a slice-and-a-half of white bread tasted like Manna to the ever hungry lads.

The Milch cows were finally tied to the fence overlooking the Thames Valley with their backs to the fire glow. The girls were glad of something to do, besides "Oh and Ah" over the blaze. They quickly filled the foaming pails. Larger boys stood at the line fence, saying soothing things—to the cows, all the while trying to ignore the girls. These girls could have stood some comforting words spoken personally to them. But it just wasn't to be.

The smaller, more excitable "Barefoot Boys" were ordered away—into the playground, lest they excite the animals.

In the months to come, many adjustments would have to be made with the produce of the 1200 acres of rich land. At the bend of the river the rich alluvial lands produced freely. Far off in the distance the "Hogsback" loomed up like the "White Cliffs of Dover."

Rich orchards heavily laden with fruit, along with berries, called for quick action. These River Flats were like "The garden of the Lord to the hungry eye of that Barefoot horde."

Vegetables had to be stored in some new place while the rich hay, Alsike, and Timothy were piled in the fields, specially topped to shed the frequent rains.

Of course, plans would soon be made to rebuild the barns with metal siding and roofs, but all that was in the future.

There was little sleep in Mt. Elgin that night for the staff or students. The Senior Staff remained on the scene, containing the embers. The younger barefoot lads enjoyed all the publicity and the excitement, and they snickered far into the night.

Across the Great Gulf the girls in their beds were disturbed by the flickering lights which shone on the walls and ceiling. They flared up at times as half-burned timber fell into the fire-bed.

Perchance in later years, when the Mt. Elgin Grads had grown to take their place as men and women with the race, they would meet again. Perhaps as fruit pickers near Jordan's Big Valley; or as Comrades-in-arms somewhere in France; better still it could be at a Revival Service, featuring the Manass Family Singers. They would rehash the old days in the Mt. Elgin "Mush-Hole," as they love to call it. But they would always come up with a PICTURE indelibly etched on their Memories. It was that Sunday afternoon, during World War I, when the Institution Barns went up in smoke.

That was Mt. Elgin's "Trial By Fire."

# Brown Tom
## "Has It Bad"

CHAPTER TEN

Brown Tom, in his misery of homesickness, sat directly across from sixty-five girls. But to Brown Tom, as yet, Girls simply did not exist. They were there, of course, but only on the margin of his consciousness. He took no personal interest in them. Nor did they influence him unduly. His little world was too full of boyish interests. And on that first night it was too full of misery.

Not that he did not appreciate the Feminine touch upon his life. He really did appreciate it very much. Especially the creature comforts that it brought. He liked Good Meals served by Feminine Hands. Clothes well mended. And the motherly touch of the Matron to fuss over him when he was sick.

He even liked cleanliness—to a certain extent. He did not want too much of that, however. He was a bit like the Rainy River Indians in the story. It was said that they used to pray for a stop to the incessant rains. This was so that they could get comfortably dirty again.

Brown Tom liked a lot of comfort and a little dirt along with it. What little boy does not?

But there was to come a day when all this was changed. A day came in which all this world of boyish interests lost its appeal. Fishing and wandering about no longer seemed to him the best pastimes. There came a day when Brown Tom's Chum went alone on his foraging.

Brown Tom stood watching the Milking Girls flock titteringly to the barn.

It all came about this way—this miracle of first Puppy Love. It happened in his fourteenth year. He had grown well on Institution fare and was quite tall. He was very experienced by this time and well versed in the tricks of Institution life.

One day at Dinner, he noticed that his Bread Pile was unusually thick. In fact the top Slice had quite an upward tilt. Though he was a reverent lad, his attention wandered during the Blessing. He was anxious to know what was beneath that top Slice.

Would it be a letter from home, perhaps enclosing a Dollar? No, the mail wasn't delivered that way. What could it be?

On sitting down, he at once lifted the Top Slice. A folded Note opened itself before him. It was, of course, a note from some Girl to someone at his Table. It had been put at the wrong place. After such publicity it had to be confiscated by the Officer in charge.

It was probably handed to the addressee as the long line filed out.

Now this stirring event opened a whole world of possibilities to Brown Tom. Here he saw the Grapevine at work but not as he had used it. He had seen it only from table to table and from Boy to Boy. This was across the Great Gulf that separated Boys from Girls.

For the first time he looked long and interestedly across that Gulf. He looked down the long line of Girls in Institution blue, intent on their meal. And somehow he was sorry that the note had not been for him.

Then that evening the miracle took place. It was at milking time when he was detailed to keep the cows quiet. The Girls did the milking while a Senior Boy stood by saying soothing things to the cow. Some of the animals were quite nervous. Most of the Girls pretended to be.

Florence Wawanesa was the girl whom he was protecting. As she finished milking, Florence stepped lightly away from the cow and thanked him. In a halting Iroquois accent she said: "Thank you Tom, I was so scairt. I did not know wat I was going to do."

Just a few simple words like that accompanied by a half-shy smile. Just a light brown face with the mere suggestion of a dimple. And a stray lock of hair that would not stay in place.

But the combined impact on Brown Tom was most upsetting. It struck him like the breath of Spring come to the frozen prairie. He almost rocked on his feet.

Then he became protective and big and masculine, beside this so-feminine helpless one. He tried to think of the right thing to say to pass it off grandly. But all he said was: "Oh that's alrite." His vocabulary had momentarily shrunk.

Then, taking the pail from her warm fingers, he walked to the Separator Room, with long strides. He was thinking of clever or effective things that he might have said to Florence. He seemed to be walking on stilts, though without effort.

He walked rapidly for a while and then slowed down near the Separator Room. Finally he stood still and thought—about Florence.

Funny he hadn't noticed her before. She had such a soft voice and that jerky Mohawk accent made it so appealing. It was cute to hear her pronounce her name "Wow-wannits-huh."

Funny how that stray lock of hair wouldn't stay up. Couldn't he do something about that—pin it back, or something?

So, wouldn't a Girl like that make a fine Friend? Just for friendly walking and talking. He could never get enough of her voice. Suppose he were to walk up and sit down beside her on the lawn next Visiting Hours . . . .

"Well, and what the Dickens is the Matter with you?" asked a burly Scotch voice.

With an effort Brown Tom came to and saw the towering Stockman watching him. The Separator was running empty.

He jumped guiltily and then quickly poured the milk into the tank. A lot of it slopped over the side. There was a new joy in his heart and the very air seemed full of Florence. The very grind and whirr of the Separator seemed to sound her name.

"Have a care there, Tom. Say, what's come over you? Ernie, you'd better handle that milk. Tom isn't quite himself tonight," said the Scotch voice.

Brown Tom, relieved of his duties, at once walked down to the stable door. He was thinking of several clever openings for a talk with Florence. What a pretty name. Funny he never noticed that dimple when she smiled before.

But, the Milking completed, the Girls had gone. All he heard was light laughter up the road. He caught a glimpse of blue dresses with white apron strings. He had missed her.

The huge Stockman, arms akimbo, looked down the corridor at him. Then turning to his helpers he exclaimed: "Oh boy, has he got it bad."

Had he heard that remark, Brown Tom would have denied it. It wasn't that. It was simply that a whole world of new possibilities had opened before him. Feminine companionship was so different. Florence really wasn't like the other girls at all. She was different—and so friendly and nice.

That night his Chum went alone to the village for Loaf 'n' Lard. "That Tom," he said, "he's never here when you want him."

Many were the trips he was to make alone after that. Finally he gave up in despair and chose someone to replace Brown Tom.

For Brown Tom had experienced what has come over Man at times from the beginning of Time. It was the Feminine Touch (the Eternal Feminine) coming into his life for the first time. It came upon him in a warm, intimate, appealing way. It was so strangely disturbing.

It transformed his whole outlook upon life. He noticed for the first time that his clothes were in need of care and that his hair could do with a combing. It brought strange stirrings and unrest. It turned his awkward boyish soul toward poetry and romance. His step became lighter and he unconsciously became more careful of his appearance. He wondered what she really thought of him. How could he make her think of him more kindly?

He was always on the alert to catch even a fleeting glimpse of her. He did not think it fair that the only times he met her she was surrounded by a bevy of other uninteresting girls. In such a group she seemed fine, friendly and perhaps just a little mischievous.

The opportunities for a quiet personal word with her seemed to become very scarce suddenly. He groaned when he thought of the many times he had spoken to her before the Awakening. Wasted opportunities.

He caught just enough glimpses of her after that to keep up the glow. But when she was near he could not express his pent-up Feelings to her. He became awkward and devoid of ideas or words.

When she had gone he became as fluent as a Greek Orator. He thought of the many clever things he might have said. The wisecracks and the way he might have led the conversation around to their two selves.

He tried to tell some of the other boys what she really meant to him. He spoke of her wholesome presence, of her hair, her eyes. But they had little patience for his tale. Some just walked away in disgust. Others turned on him and said: "Why don't you tell Her that?"

When the wise ones of the earth can explain the phenomena of nature, they can dissect fully the emotional awakening of Brown Tom. Nature is so full of such awakenings. Perhaps, on the other hand, it would spoil the picture to have it all explained. Is not Appreciation better than Knowledge?

The wild goose rises from the from the Northern Lakes. It wings its way South over the land of the Tumbleweed. The newly hatched turtle strikes for the water's edge, without instruction. The partridge drums his lonely call on the half-rotted log.

And Brown Tom stands watching the Milking girls flock down to the Barn of an evening. They are so absorbedly and independently happy in their group companionship. Only a sly backward look (furtive) betrays their interest in him and his Chums. That half-shy smile and the jerky Mohawk accent disturbs his thoughts.

Years after, when the symptoms of the malady were half erased, Brown Tom recognised this as Puppy Love. It was his first and most ethereal yearning: the kind that comes only once in a lifetime—and to adolescents only. It was gossamer spun, intensely disturbing. It left a residue of pleasant memory for the realistic days ahead.

One day his Chum stood watching him as he wrote. It was a note to be sent by the Grapevine system to Her across the Gulf.

At last his Chum's patience was exhausted.

"Gaw, he's got a wumman," he said. Then he went out to choose a new Chum.

# Brown Tom Gets Religion

## CHAPTER ELEVEN

Brown Tom was very religious. His school religion began right after breakfast at Morning Prayers. This consisted of the Hymn, Scripture and Medium-long Prayers. Through it all the Boys thought of their limited breakfast, and the period till noon seemed endless. Of course, there were the usual comments on the Day's outline of work. Sometimes three or four boys were given a special task, like pumping water into the attic tank.

The hymns by this time were familiar and the Prayers were relaxing—the Scripture was read without comment. Sometimes Brown Tom's attention wandered.

If someone had blundered, attention was drawn to the fact. He was held up as a terrible example of "How Not To Behave." Occasionally the culprit was called by name and ominously asked to "remain."

As soon as he was later released from the Office his Chums flocked around him. They examined his red hands and asked in awed tones: "Gaw. How many did you get?"

In response, he first looked carefully around, then he boastfully shouted, as he ran toward the barn: "Oh, I'm a tough guy. They can't hurt me."

Evening prayers were much after the same pattern. Occasionally an address was given by one of the Officers or by some visiting V.I.P.

To all this religious programme Brown Tom submitted. It did not, however, have a very profound effect upon his developing life. School religion was like that, so he made the best of it. Sometimes the more familiar and appealing hymns "stuck in their crops," and the boys who heard them sang as they worked: "There's Sunshine in my soul today," or "The Eye is on the Sparrow."

White man's religion was something that Indians took along with White man's oversight, and later, White man's liquor. It was all a part of the same package, though an appealing part.

One evening Brown Tom did take an active part in this religious programme. He often wondered who the Principal was talking to during the longer prayers. Maybe it was like Santa Claus whom no-one saw. Maybe he shouldn't see him either.

Curiosity got the better of his judgement, so as he sat bowed "in reverence crouched," we should say, beside Helm Goodleaf, he leaned out into the aisle and looked up at the front. He expected to see God there, to whom the Principal was speaking.

But all he saw was the tall figure of the Principal and the electric lights covered by inverted sugar bowls. He quickly closed his eyes and never told anyone about what he didn't see. But he wondered.

On Sunday, in addition to these regular Prayers, there was Church Parade. It was a nice walk along dusty roads through "beau pays" to a vine-covered church.

This was more interesting. The dressing-up part of it had an especial appeal. From time to time the Principal would buy up a job lot of Boys suits. They smelled faintly of woodsmoke, but sometimes one got a fair fitting.

So, here we see Brown Tom all dressed up in a grey suit with knee pants. On his head was a light-fitting cap with a diminutive peak and topped off with a cloth-covered button. He felt quite dressed up in his "Sunday, go-to-meeting" clothes.

The girls, accompanied (chaperoned) by the Officers, walked ahead down the dusty road. On either side were luxurious growths of vines and berry bushes showing through the rail fences. The trees were mostly hardwoods and of varying heights.

Next to the Girls came the Little Boys, pushing and quarrelling among themselves. Then came the Big Boys with all the soberness and authority of their years.

There was subdued chatter along the line as the march progressed. Chums asked each other about yesterday's outing and future plans. There were special cliques and common interests as among small-town citizens.

As they neared the rustic church the chatter died down. Only one piping voice carried on. It was asking insistently some "Jake" the exact location of some newfound apple trees.

When the Officer's "Shush" produced no silencing effect, one of the Senior Boys called out in a loud stage whisper: "Pipe down, Muskrat. What d'you think this is? Gundgeon?"

It had the desired result.

Then quickly the subdued line marched into the church.

The Church service followed the usual order and was conducted by a saintly "son o' Glasgae." During it all, the girls sat quietly attentive. Boys outwardly attentive, but only pretending.

The officers sprayed the lines with stern gaze, on the alert for any misbehaviour. Who was it said the Laws were made for the Lawbreakers and not for the Righteous?

They joined heartily in the singing and only the furtive pinch on the side of a chum's leg showed they were not all attention. In the prayers all were very quiet while some traced the lines between the flooring boards or watched a ladybug crawling along. Most of them wondered about the size of the "Sunday Cake" to come.

The Collection Plate, of course, was not passed to them, but they took a keen interest in the coins falling into it. Any one of those coins would have provided a Feast of Loaf 'n' Lard.

Sunday School followed at 2 p.m. Here the hymns were more swingy and cheerful, and the Bible stories held most of their attention. Of course the miracles were hard for a little boy to understand. But then it had all happened so long ago.

Brown Tom submitted to this Religious Programme. Was he not a Ward of the Government? He accepted their Religion along with the handouts of clothing, food and shelter. He sometimes wondered if the Longhouse religion back home wasn't as satisfying as this.

He remembered how his people back on the Reserve had submitted in the same unquestioning way. The missionary came and did his thing; conducting regular services at designated points. Each one discouraged the Longhouse religion and the use of native language. They were being weaned away from the native culture, as though it had no spiritual or aesthetic value. They would have been shocked to hear a native teacher speak of a song in the Mohawk Language as "the sweetest music this side of Heaven." Indian languages were not heard about the Institution. Occasionally Indian might be spoken in a low voice or some naughty uncouth native word might be used by the younger chaps.

These early missionaries were devout and sincere. They had a task to perform and they carried it out. A lot of them lacked any special training for the task; the majority of them lacked imagination. Many considered the Indian work as a backward step, and performed their duties in the hope of an opening in the "regular work."

Brown Tom's parents' generation went along with all this gracefully. They washed their faces and put on stiff starched collars. They donned their blue serge suits that they had earned picking berries or cutting wood. Then they marched down to the Church.

Certain things about Church appealed to them. They liked to sing—tho' not too fast. They loved to "sway" as they sang. Especially in certain pieces like "On the Happy Golden Shore." Then, too, the lead had to wait for the deep Bass, which believed it was fashionable to be late. The Bass took its time but rattled the shingles when it arrived.

They liked "special occasions." Especially Christmas and New Year's, when they could decorate the old Church. It was drab the greater part of the year, so they might be excused if they rather overdid it. They dragged in the old pine Christmas tree and made a "Merry Christmas" sign with pine boughs sewed onto cardboard.

That generation respected the Church, the Cloth, and Religion. They felt that these had meant a lot to their elders whom they loved.

Years later, there was to come to Brown Tom's Reserve, the ideal Indian Missionary. By accident of birth he was Anglo-Saxon, but his love embraced all humanity, with its colours, creeds and varieties of culture.

He came because he wanted to come, burning his bridges behind him. He and his consecrated wife decided to live among these new friends as unreservedly as did the missionaries to the Chinese and the Hindu. There was to be no looking back and no vain regrets.

Where love is, of course, one gives all.

For them there was no "Indian Problem." There was only a Human Problem. That Problem was to get these new friends "Off Relief."

Out in the Dustbowl and in the wretched parts of great cities they had seen the demoralizing effects of years of Relief. There the problem was to teach the people "How To Go Off Relief Gracefully." The Problem here was the same, only more intensified. For the Indian people had been On Relief, so to speak, for three hundred years. Those people had only been demoralized by it for ten years.

Among outside Reliefers he had found unfortunate tendencies. These were laziness, carelessness in personal appearance, and not too high a regard for the truth. On the Reserve he found these same general tendencies, only more deeply engrained from longer exposure. It was not surprising. It was a result of the system of paternalism. Not all Reliefers degenerated. Neither did all Indians. Among both peoples were found upright characters. Their heads were "bloody but unbowed"; their souls were not for sale.

So he took a stout stick and went for a walk through the Reserve. His aim was just to be friendly and humane. He met with a ready response. When the men were baling hay he stopped and chatted. He helped weigh bundles and even loosened some of the hay where it was binding along the stack edges. He remained to Dinner and after the work enjoyed potatoes fixed with turnips and smothered in rich gravy. He asked the Blessing when called upon to do so.

And horrors. He attended an Indian Square Dance following a Wood-Cutting Bee. His wife was there, surrounded by young girls who were in her CG [CGIT] group. These youngsters were caught up in a stream of Indian custom and flocked to her as a refuge in a storm.

He had an old Slide Lantern purchased on the Instalment Plan. Occasionally he showed missionary slides or had a Hymn Slide Service (Song) at the different points. He found that he had to use an "A" Wet Battery as the Reserve was off the Hydro line.

Again he used it for Adult Education, showing free Government or Railway Slides. There was an immediate response to these special services. Those who came soon developed the habit of regular Church attendance. He used a special bulb, and an Indian mechanic with a windcharger kept his battery up.

Of course, he organized CGIT and Tuxis work for the youngsters. He had a YPS group at each appointment, which were well attended. It was something to take the place of the Square Dance.

Then when Summer came around he challenged them to have a camp for Indians only. There was a splendid Campsite on the shores of a small Reserve Lake. The equipment, tents, etc. he borrowed wherever he could, on and off the Reserve. Camp Mothers and Cooks were easy to locate and handymen were willing to do the rough work.

That first Camp had 51 Boys and the one the week following had 65 Girls. It was run along Depression lines. No regular cash charge was made but each child was given a list of things to bring, mostly garden produce. This improved the gardening very much for the following year.

So the Summer Camp became an annual affair.

Around the Campfire at night they sang both secular and sacred, and Indian as well as English songs. They took naturally to the Outdoor life, Campcraft and Handiwork.

And the Torchlight procession at the Closing Ceremony was a most impressive affair. It awakened in them far-off dim echoes of other days. Did not their far-removed ancestors enjoy the mystery of fire, and the quietness of a lakeside at night?

You see, he was an Ideal Indian missionary. So he believed that what was good for the Anglo-Saxon was not too good for the Ojibwa. He planned later to have a consolidated Church. It was to be a Community Centre where Religion in all its phases would have ample scope for expression.

So, because his Minister was friendly and human and helpful, because his Church life had spice and variety as well as depth, and because Church groups were organized for all stages of life and growth, Brown Tom and all the other "Brown Toms" really "got religion."

# The Roar of Mighty Waters

## CHAPTER TWELVE

The Institute was well situated at the head of the Muskegan River, on a high plateau. In summer it gave good view of rich farm lands on both sides of the river. In the flats there could be seen farming operations in full swing, which was handy for the Overseer, who could see it all at a glance without seeming to spy on the young toilers.

At the end of the valley ran a railway line crossing an iron bridge and high embankment. In winter, ploughs could be seen bringing furnace coal from the rail yards. A smaller wooden bridge for horse-drawn vehicles crossed the river.

Just below the school at the river bend was the boys' swimming hole. With its muddy bottom and murky waters, it was where many a lad first learned to float and swim. This swimming, of course, was done without benefit of swimming togs. They swam "in the raw" as they expressed it, being well out of sight from the school and from travellers along the dusty bush road.

But the Spring with "ice break-up time" brought the most interesting and spectacular sights. For this river, which in July became a shallow fordable stream, was in Spring a huge lake spreading across the whole valley.

All the water from northern melting snow, with fallen trees and bits of buildings, floated along with the huge jagged dirty blocks of ice. Often these muddy, jagged blocks roared and crashed against each other, heaving one up above the others. Small buildings and huge trees whirled and twisted around all the other floating debris.

It was the spring break-up after a long hard winter.

On such occasions, between suppertime and Evening Prayers, the whole population of the school lined up against the fence that ran along the top of the precipice. The girls, who had quite a shut-in life, enjoyed these outings, and their shrill cries mingled with the deeper voices of the boys, at the variety of sights to be seen.

"Oh, look it, the Backhouse," shouted wee Abe Muskrat, as a small building floated by with the ice.

"Shush," said senior boy Norman Brosette, "you mean 'Water Closet,'" as he turned to see if the girls had heard Abe's outcry. These older boys never knew what uncouth remark the younger lads would be coming out with.

Sometimes these small buildings carried a hen perched on top riding with the flotsam. Rails from some farmyard, or lumber from a sawmill rolled and tossed with the turbulent flow.

The fishing prospects when the waters subsided were a favourite subject of conversation with the boys. Fish could be sold at the kitchen for one cent per pound, which would help pay for Feasts.

One evening when the floods were at their worst, the Principal called the Instructors together for a conference. He was concerned about the cattle on the flats, as the waste waters were rising and driving the cattle against the pasture fence. There was not time to drive the long way around to rescue the cattle.

The Carpenter Foreman, Norman Waubouse, an Abenaki from Gat Valley, offered to row the boat across the wild floods to rescue the cattle. The senior boys crowded to volunteer to help and three of the largest boys, from various reserves, were chosen. When the kitchen leaders saw what was planned, they bustled up to ask Mr. Mack not to allow it. But there was no time for delay.

The boat was launched, the foreman rowed at the rear and a senior boy sat in front; two others sat between them with stout poles to hold back the floating blocks of ice and debris.

As the sun sank lower in the west, the school crowd and adult leaders leaned against the fence to watch the brave and dangerous rescue.

Cries of dismay and horror came from female throats as large blocks of ice studded with tree branches bore down on the boat, now only dimly seen across the waters. But the boat made its tortuous way to the bawling and milling cows. At times the boat was out of sight behind trees or parts of the building and cries of concern went up from the female sector watchers.

As the sun went down behind the high railway embankment, the small boat on the large expanse of flood landed safely on the small area where the cattle were crowded together. The wire fence was cut and a wide gate thrown open, through which the cows crowded together in their anxiety to escape.

"Oh, I hope they don't try to row back," exclaimed the Senior Girls. "Don't be foolish," advised the boys, "they will probably camp across there overnight."

But there was no need to worry. As the officials talked together and planned their safe return, the stockman was seen hitching a pair of fast horses to the two-seater democrat which soon disappeared down the river road in a cloud of dust. At a sign from the Principal the girls were herded back into the school with the boys sauntering behind them to their Playroom.

Very ardent Prayers of Thanksgiving were offered that evening for the safety of the boys and their leaders from across the mighty waters. The boys made motions of rowing under the desk, as they imagined themselves heroes-to-be.

The river played a large part in the lives of the Feathered Urchins. It was an interesting spectacle at flood time, a swimming hole on hot summer evenings, and a source of revenue for boys who caught a variety of fish in the lowered waters, with their many hooked lines.

The outlay of only a few cents bought them fishline and hooks, while earthworms and grubs were there for the digging. The kitchen paid one cent a pound for these fish, which then found their way, nicely browned, to the dinner table. No sales pitch was needed for this deal. All a boy had to do was tap gently on the kitchen door and hold up a mullet in a grubby hand, without comment. The cook took it, weighed it, and handed out a few pennies which were safely deposited in an overalls pocket.

The boys who chose fishing as their hobby got fisherman's luck, which from time immemorial has been described as "a wet backside and a belly full of hunger."

They stole down to the river at every moment that was not full of school duties and the call of the Bell. On cool, damp mornings they tied a red horseshoe sinker to the end of their fish lines, and every three feet a baited hook. They then whirled the iron sinker around their heads, throwing it well into the centre of the river. Then they hustled back to the Playroom before the first Bell for Prayers called one and all.

On their next visit to their lines they pulled out a variety of denizens of the deep on their hooks. Here would be found a mullet or sucker, with the odd large black catfish (bullheads), maybe a turtle, a shiny squirmy eel and other fishy items. They threw away the useless ones, and taking the edible fish they made a beeline for the kitchen. With the few coppers paid to them, they forgot all the cold, the dampness and the misery of the fisherman's lot, in the prospect of a 10 cent feast coming up.

# Happy Hunting Ground for Noah

## CHAPTER THIRTEEN

The milling herd existed within four grey walls, the four grey towers of the Institution, and spilled over occasionally into the local White man's world. They were generally sound healthy creatures.

Of course there were a lot of common colds, running noses which were duly wiped on smock sleeves, and sores on their faces and ears that were covered by white salve. Then there were the digestive upsets from eating half-frozen apples or too much "Loaf 'n' Lard." The girls, of course, were always "getting sick" as the boys disgustedly exclaimed.

But occasionally the silent killer, TB, showed up amongst the enrolment. Some quiet, inoffensive lad would grow unusually quiet and listless. One such victim was young Noah. He would be found sitting alone down by the riverside pretending to fish. But his mind was clouded with many questions and doubts.

He would remember how prone Indian people were to get TB. He had seen white isolation tents standing outside the homes of sick people. Even the White people who worked the stone quarry sometimes had such tents. As he tied an extra hook to his fish line his memory floated back to the Sunday School lesson: "as prone as the sparks to fly upward. . . ."

The whirls of Institution life went on around him—the pairs who went to the village for feasts, the love notes passing across the Great Gulf, apple stealing, the fist fights and the passing of Sunday Cake to pay a debt. All this went on and more, but Noah kept his thoughts to himself and avoided getting involved in any of these things.

Finally he reported sick. The concerned Matron bustled around taking his temperature and cooking special soups. When the Principal walked by he took one look and said to Miss McTaggart, "We had better call Dr. Holmes, this could be serious."

"You mean . . . ?" she said.

"Yes," said the Principal, "I mean just that—TB."

Noah had been quite an active boy, though he was never interested in rough or rowdy play. He was more of the spectator type, always interested in the doings of his young friends.

He sometimes fished quietly, but was more often seen on the river bank in the afternoons making a slingshot or a wooden gun to which an archer's bow was attached. The boys called this a "Bow-gun-arrow." He spent a lot of time at home as his Reserve lay just across the river. Sometimes he took a chum home with him for some home-cooked "grub."

But as his creeping, insidious disease came over him, he began to lose interest in all boyish activity. He coughed frequently and his energy was sapped away. His chums tried to interest him in their games and outings, but he only smiled wanly and told them to leave him out. He didn't feel like it.

Soon after this Noah was taken away from the Institution quietly, and emptiness remained where the gentle boy had lived with his pals.

# War Clouds Over Mt. Elgin

## CHAPTER FOURTEEN

The Institute life seemed remote, calm and sequestered from the outside world. The Roar of the White man's Rivalry in Commerce and World Status resulting in war should have reached them, but they heard only a far-off distant echo.

But by September 1914, war clouds from Europe had filtered into even this sheltered spot. Letters from home told of older brothers "joining up" and "donning khaki" (Cake-eye), and doing their bit for King and pays. Sometimes it was Dad who had enlisted.

They really didn't know what it all meant. But some good came out of it when dollar bills began to be enclosed more often with letters from home. They began to hear about the "Separation Allowance" paid their Moms, and the $1 a day paid to Dad who shouldered a Ross Rifle. In their history lessons they learned where the "red BRITISH line" was. And they wondered if Dad or Brother was there among all the White folks.

Little did they know that Dad was still in the "awkward squad," trying to "form fours" and to spit out tobacco and gum before lining up. Of course the Indian bandsmen were swankier than the regular soldiers with swagger sticks under their arms, and the knowledge that their uniform was a passport to many grand homes that had heretofore been closed to them.

In the fall of 1914 the war was often mentioned at Evening Prayers. The war meant a lot to the Staff—especially since most of them were Irish Methodists. They too had reports of their relatives joining up, and some were lost in army and navy accidents. They had a great sense of Geography, but this was not the case for the feathered urchins who thought it all seemed very far away.

To try to rectify this situation and involve the children more, the staff introduced military and patriotic songs. These songs were new to the youngsters but were to stay with them to the end of their days. These war songs were played on a scratchy old gramophone after Prayers and the students were urged to join in. Amongst the songs were "Keep the Home Fires Burning—while your hearts are yearning," and "Pack all Your Troubles." They heard how the troops, both Indian and White, were called in from the "Hillside, the Heather, and the Glen." Others that followed were "We'll never let the Old Flag Fall, for we have it best of all."

Union Jacks were put up to decorate the Prayer Room and offices. Of course the flags were already familiar to the students, as every school on every Reserve had them displayed prominently.

It was not long before Missionaries appeared in military uniform and were the toast of the evening. Their shiny brass buttons, blackened shoes, and light military belt gave them a very trim and snappy appearance. But all too soon these men disappeared, only to appear later in the casualty lists.

But it was when one of their own kind was reported joining the army that the War became a personal thing. The son of a famous Chief from a nearby Reserve was among the first to join up. Later they heard about recent Mt. Elgin graduates who had joined up. These names were added weekly to a Roll of Honour that was posted prominently above the Prayer Room Platform. There was no distinction of race on it, with the names of relatives and friends of both staff and students intertwined. It was no longer simply a White man's war. War had welded the soldiers into one national group. Canadians all.

Brown Tom and his chums wondered what it was like and what it was all about. They took more interest in the "red British line" as they wondered what was happening to the soldiers they knew. The war was beginning to touch them in real and personal ways.

# Brown Tom "Arrives"

## CHAPTER FIFTEEN

The slowly revolving wheel of Time brought Brown Tom, in his fifteenth year, to Graduation. Brown Tom had "arrived," in a scholastic sense. Having passed the successive yearly exams, he could proceed no further at the Institution schools.

Behind him lay four years of Institution life with all its mosaic of delight and grief. The time had come for the solo flight that each Indian graduate must make, away from the Institution walls.

When he looked back in later years, these four years were studded with many pleasant memories. He recalled the twelve hundred acres of rich farm land basking in the Summer sunshine. Its soil was rich and its products luscious, "Fair as a garden of the Lord, To the eyes of that famished rebel horde."

He also recalled many pleasant outings. There was the gathering of walnuts when the first frosts of Autumn had turned the leaves to a golden glow. His fingers had been a jaundiced yellow from the juice of the crushed rinds.

He remembered too the warm Spring days, when, on free afternoons, they had lain in the rank grass of the alluvial flats and had argued by the hour. In the Spring they had fished with a horseshoe sinker and six temptingly baited hooks. All these happy experiences lay behind him in his final year.

One Sunday afternoon, during Visiting Hours, the Senior Class was assembled on the lawn. The wide-spreading maples afforded a good shade and the well-kept lawns a good cushion. They were indeed a motley crowd of boys and girls, coming from many different Reserves. Here were Angus Shewung, Mitchell Noash, Alvira Half-Moon, Bessie Ashleaf, Adam Gibson, Lottie Laframe, Welby Roundsky, and Brown Tom.

The girls sat on the grass toying with each others' hair ribbon bows. They would put their arms around each other and look across at the boys. The boys sprawled awkwardly in various ungainly poses, roughly pushing each other around.

"Lay off my foot, you big walrus," said Adam to Welby. "You must weigh at least a ton."

"Look here, fellows," said Mitchell, "we must be serious. This may be the last chance we'll have to be together and there's a lot to discuss. Our people are in bondage to the White man, and their Rights are denied them. We who have some education ought to help them. They ought to get back the land, money and rights that have been stolen from them. Why, I know a reserve . . . ."

Angus let out a groan and cried, "He's at it again. Stop him somebody before I see Red and grab a tomahawk or something."

"You wouldn't know what to do with one if you had it," said Bessie. "You boys would make a fine bunch of warriors."

"Well, we could still drag our women home by the hair," retorted Welby.

"You're thinking of cavemen, not Indians," said Brown Tom. "Get your story straight."

It was Spring. The world of Nature was lush and beautiful. They were each in their own way youthful and aspiring. After these last few days it would be the parting of the ways. They would each work out their own destinies according to the personal trend.

"Seriously tho," said Alvira. "What're you big clumsy boys going to make of yourselves when you get back to the Reserve? Now, me, I'd like to be a nurse. I'd go on the Reserve and heal and soothe all their little hurts. It bothers me to see those little gaffers come to the matron with their scratches to be healed and their slivers to be pulled. They come in here with their long black hair hanging into their eyes and with scars on their ears and faces. Oh there's so much good to be done."

"You can start nursing me," said Adam. "I got me a pain right here in my tummy."

"Cheer up Adam," said Alvira. "Supper will cure your pain and when you get home you can have all the gundgeon bread you want."

"Me," said Welby, "I'm gonna be a farmer. And I mean a farmer—a real up-to-date come-and-get-it type. I'm gonna show them back there how to grow some real purebred stock. Any old cow as long as it can hold together won't be good enough for me. Instead of going out to work in the canning factory or on the fruit farms, I'll show them how to farm right. I'll . . ."

"Yes, you'll show them, won't you," said Lottie. "I'll bet your purebred cows will be bawling for their breakfasts before you get up. You won't have the old bell to call you then, you know."

"Oh I'll let the wife feed them," retorted he. "Whatsa use a havin' a woman around the place if she can't feed cows?"

Mitchell, the stern Nationalist, could keep quiet no longer: "What's the use of all this if the Indians are themselves to be treated like dumb driven cattle? I know a Reserve where, by a Treaty, they were promised all the land along a river from its source to its mouth. Today they are huddled in a mere fraction of that."

"Well Mitchell," said Adam. "You go hunt up the treaties. I am gonna be busy makin' a livin.'"

There was a healthy camaraderie between these High School boys and girls. It was not the romantic love of the earlier years, nor was it the crude sensual interest that so often creeps in. They were just loyal friends who found it pleasant to be together.

They did their Homework together and often took time off to argue problems of Reserve Life. This group would soon be breaking up to go their several ways. In the nature of the case there could be no hope of a future Class Reunion.

"You know," said Adam, "I've got it all over the rest of you. I've got a trade, and I don't mean maybe. I'm a carpenter like my Dad only a better one. I'm better because I can read an' write. He couldn't do either but he built some pretty fine houses. I face the world with my box of tools. I'll work anywhere on or off the Reserve, for anybody, black, white, red or yellow. That's me all over."

Lottie was gently pulling a sweet clover head apart. She said quietly: "I want to be a Teacher. I am going back on the Reserve to help. They need me there. I am going to Normal and get fully qualified. And I want to teach Sunday School as well as Day School."

"Hurrah, Lottie's got Religion," shouted Angus, until she beat him over the head with a Sunday School paper.

"No, I believe even one person could do a lot of good . . . look at all the Religion we've been exposed to here. Some of the kids on the Reserve never see the inside of a Sunday School," she said.

Welby hit Angus a resounding whack and said, "Wake up Mohawk, what's your great ambition in life?"

Angus roared in mock agony and, rolling on his back with his hat on his eyes, said: "My one great ambition in life, when I get out of this Mush 'n' Milk Jail, is to get me one good square meal."

The group rocked with laughter, amid cries of "Attaboy, Angus." The girls looked at one another and said, "What an ambition."

Angus sat up saying, "No, I really mean it. I want a real he-man meal of gundgeon bread, potatoes boiled with their skins on, some real fat pork and Thick Man's gravy."

"You mean 'Poor Man's Gravy,'" said Alvira, "made with flour and browned over a hot fire. Better stop, Angus, you're makin' Tom Hungry."

"Makin'," said Brown Tom. "Say, I've been hungry for four years. But listen you high aimers. Let me tell you my ambition. I am staying with the books. Books have made me what I am."

"Why blame the books?" said Mitchell, lying with his cap over his face.

Brown Tom went on unheeding: "Remember old Zerk telling us about his College days—all that Rah Rah Rah stuff? The books may lead me to all that. I want to get my matriculation and 'follow knowledge like a sinking star' . . . "

". . . or something," added Angus.

His speech was interrupted by the ringing of the Supper Bell. Adam sprang to his feet and dramatically waving his arms exclaimed: "Akwekon Kwahonkara wis imtisaway tasea watskaho."

Alvira, who had half risen, sank down again and asked in astonishment, "My goodness, what outlandish language is that?"

Welby looked at her a moment and said: "That's good Mohawk for 'come and eat.' Let's go." Whereupon he pulled her to her feet. The group scattered in a ready response.

The day of Graduation finally arrived. It was the strangest Graduation that beast or bird had ever seen. It might well have been called a Commencement exercise, because it was for that class the beginning of a new and untried life.

They had come to these portals as Ontario Indians. They were leaving it as world citizens. They only asked the chance to make their contribution to the world's progress.

The valedictory of that class was like nothing before or since. Usually a school can say to its graduates: "We have trained and equipped you for the battle of life. The world is your oyster to open as you can. Go out into the world and make good."

This school could not say that however. The Principal said: "I have tried to develop in each of you a sound mind within a sound body. Wherever your lot is cast, that will stand you in good stead."

These graduates had only been brought to the parting of the ways. The school could lead them no further, nor advise them which road to take. The one road was an unpromising but familiar and well-worn one. It led back to the Reserve life. The other was a bright upland way, but beset by many uncertainties. It led out to the great Anglo-Saxon world of competition and continuous struggle.

There were two lions at the gateway of this latter road. The one was subjective, the other objective. They were an inferiority complex on the one hand, and real narrow race-prejudice on the other.

One wonders what were the private thoughts and emotions of the Staff on that day. Were they satisfied with their work, or did doubts assail them? Surely no Instructors of the Past had ever been given such a task? Under the circumstances they had done their best. It was now to be sink or swim in the lone outing of graduation from these walls.

The doubts that might have assailed them would be these: they had trained these youngsters in the White man's ways, given them White man's education. Had this all been a mistake? Had these gifts not only served to unfit them for the old Reserve life without being able to promise them very much out in the great big Anglo-Saxon world? Had it been for better or worse?

Whatever the answer, on many Indian Reserves today, there are Indian senior citizens who have that Sunday afternoon in June indelibly etched in their memories. For they were in the "Class of Mt. Elgin 1915."

# Afterword

*Mary I. Anderson and Margaret McKenzie*

Enos Montour would have been gratified to know his work in *Brown Tom's Schooldays* was quoted in the Truth and Reconciliation Commission report. He would also have been delighted to know his granddaughters collaborated with his former editor, Elizabeth Graham, and with Mary Jane Logan McCallum to reprint *Brown Tom's Schooldays*.

Enos was the youngest of four boys born to Elijah and Mary Montour. When Enos was two years old, Mary died tragically, leaving Elijah to raise the family with his parents' assistance. Money was scarce and Elijah would leave home for long periods to seek work. When Elijah was told his youngest sons had to attend the Mount Elgin Residential School at Muncey, Ontario, there was little argument.

Many of Enos's family recall hearing stories of the "Mush Hole," the nickname given to Mount Elgin. A common theme in the stories was a lack of food and being hungry to the point that several young boys would steal into the vegetable storage shed to hollow out and eat raw turnip. Enos expressed mixed emotions about Residential School life. He loved learning and was a lifelong learner, as evidenced by books he read and CBC radio programs he listened to. In later years, he acknowledged that the school offered a certain amount of stability that he would not have had at home. However, the school deprived him of his culture. He once said that when he returned to Six Nations, the reserve did not feel like home but neither was the outside world.

After his days at Residential School, Enos worked at various jobs. During one summer at the end of the First World War, he went to Saskatchewan to work on a farm. There was a need for farm help, as many young men had been recruited from the prairie provinces to fight in the war. The 1918 pandemic had also taken its toll. As Enos told it, he was working for one of the staunchest Methodist families in the area, and this would be a turning point that would eventually see Enos entering McGill University. The Methodist Church at that time was very interested in recruiting Indigenous men who would be willing to minister to other Indigenous people.

In 1925, Enos was accepted into McGill and by 1929 had graduated with Bachelor of Arts and Bachelor of Divinity degrees. In 1929, he was required to do a student internship at Maniwaki, Quebec, under the supervision of the Reverend George Lalond. While there, Reverend Lalond's sister-in-law was visiting and caught the eye of the young student minister. Hilda Hanna and Enos were married that spring.

When Enos was ordained, there were no vacancies in Indigenous communities, so he and Hilda moved to Ceylon, Saskatchewan. This would be the beginning of many moves, as the United Church had a policy that their ministers must move every four years to a new posting. (In 1925, the Methodist Church of Canada, about 70 percent of Presbyterian congregations, and the groups known as Congregationalists and Unionists agreed to become one church known as the United Church of Canada.)

During their second post, Hilda and Enos learned about a baby girl being given up for adoption by an unwed mother. Shirley became part of the family. When she was nine years old, Enos was called back to Ontario to Six Nations. With the help of his brother Nathan and various people of Ohsweken, they would revive the Chapel of the Delaware, now known as the Chapel of the Delaware United Church.

In 1953, Enos was called to a small town in southern Saskatchewan. Shirley had just finished high school and moved with her parents. It was here at Aneroid that she met her future husband, William McKenzie, the son of Scottish pioneer farmers. Enos and Hilda were thrilled to gain a son-in-law and eventually two grand-daughters. The Montours made many trips to the farm and especially enjoyed helping with meals and childcare at harvest time.

In 1965, Enos retired and they moved to Moose Jaw, Saskatchewan. In 1972, Hilda passed away, and two years later, Enos chose to move to a retirement home in Beamsville, Ontario, for United Church ministers and families. Here he met his second wife, Florence McNair, with whom he spent several years of companionship. In 1975, Enos was bestowed with an Honorary Doctorate of Divinity from McGill University for his work in the church and with Indigenous people. In 1982, he began collaborating with Elizabeth Graham on *Brown Tom's Schooldays*. He lived long enough to see it published in 1984.

Enos was passionate about his Indigenous roots, as witnessed by his writings in *The Feathered U.E.L.'s*, *Brown Tom's Schooldays*, and *The Rockhound of New Jerusalem*, as well as numerous journal and newspaper articles. He also had strong feelings of loyalty toward the British monarchy that led him to obtain United Empire Loyalist status. It was this same loyalty that had brought his ancestors to the land along the Grand River in southern Ontario.

Growing up, we did not understand what it meant that our grand-father had attended a Residential School. We always knew that he was a Delaware from Six Nations in Ontario, but for us he was just Grandpa Montour, a loving, kind, and gentle person with a lively sense of humour. He was a wonderful storyteller and encouraged us to read and learn about the world. He loved small animals, especially cats, which he called shoomocksees; dogs were affectionately referred to as "smelly pooches." One tradition of his we recall was that he always had some kind of pit or stove in the backyard where he would have a campfire. He loved to sit and gaze into the glowing embers. The most memorable of these was when he built a firepit within Hilda's rose arbour.

In 1986, the United Church of Canada offered an apology for its role in the Residential School system. We wonder what Enos's response would have been, but it is Brown Tom's reflections in the last chapter that may have presaged his answer.

We want to thank Elizabeth Graham and Mary Jane Logan McCallum for their contributions to have *Brown Tom's Schooldays* reprinted. It is our hope that this book will be one more step toward truth and reconciliation. In Enos's words: Onagi wahi (I *have* spoken).

Mary I. Anderson
Margaret McKenzie
July 2022

# Glossary of Idioms
# and References in
# *Brown Tom's Schooldays*

## APPENDIX 1

### FROM THE BIBLE

| Phrase | Reference | Page |
| --- | --- | --- |
| as prone . . . as the sparks fly upward | Job 5:7 | 143 |
| baptism of fire | Matthew 3:11 | 83 |
| garden of the Lord | Isaiah 51:3 | 147 |
| the Great Temptation | various | 104 |
| a Great Gulf was fixed; across the Great Gulf | Luke 16:26 | 103, 123, 126, 143 |
| in reverence crouched | Genesis | 132 |
| Laws were made for the Lawbreakers | Timothy 1:9–11 | 133 |
| little Indian Esaus . . . a mess of pottage | Genesis 25:29–34 | 104 |
| Morning of Time | Job 38:6 | 104 |
| Wise Men . . . who being warned in a dream had returned another way | Matthew 2:1–12 | 82 |

POETRY

| Phrase | Source | Author | Date | Page |
|---|---|---|---|---|
| an aching void | "Walking with God" | William Cowper | 1772 | 101 |
| the Barefoot Boy | "The Barefoot Boy" | John Greenleaf Whittier | 1855 | 118 |
| bloody but unbowed | "Invictus" | William Ernest Henley | 1888 | 136 |
| called the cattle home [and] across the sands of Dee | "The Sands of Dee" | Charles Kingsley | 1850 | 118–22 |
| dark hour alone; having his dark hour alone | "The Dark Night of the Soul" | St. John of the Cross | 1542–1591 | 88, 106, 109, 117 |
| the endless toil and endeavour of life | "The Day Is Done" | Henry Wadsworth Longfellow | 1844 | 90 |
| Fair as a garden of the Lord / To the eyes of that famished rebel horde | "Barbara Frietchie" | John Greenleaf Whittier | 1863 | 147 |
| follow knowledge like a sinking star | "Ulysses" | Alfred, Lord Tennyson | 1842 | 152 |
| In the stormy East wind straining | "The Lady of Shalott" | Alfred, Lord Tennyson | 1832 | 75 |
| Just before sunrise, the cold clear hours | "The Return of the Swallows" | Sir Edmund William Gosse | 1849 | 75 |

| | | | | |
|---|---|---|---|---|
| sleep that wakes in laughing day | "The Barefoot Boy" | John Greenleaf Whittier | 1855 | 118 |
| The toad beneath the harrow; also a 13th-century saying meaning "sufferers" | "Pagett, M.P." | Rudyard Kipling | 1886 | xii |
| What's so rare as a day in June | *The Vision of Sir Launfal* (book) | James Russell Lowell | 1848 | 76 |

## SONGS

| *Phrase* | *Source* | *Author* | *Page* |
|---|---|---|---|
| The Eye is on the Sparrow | "His Eye Is on the Sparrow" | Civilla D. Martin and Charles H. Gabriel | 132 |
| Hark the Herald | "Hark the Herald Angels Sing" | Christmas carol | 108 |
| Hillside, the Heather and the Glen | "Keep the Home Fires Burning Till the Boys Come Home" | Leslie Guibert Ford and Ivor Novello | 145 |
| Keep the Home Fires Burning—while your hearts are yearning | "Keep the Home Fires Burning Till the Boys Come Home"" | Leslie Guilbert Ford and Ivor Novello | 145 |
| The Little Old Sod Shanty on the Claim | "The Little Old Sod Shanty on the Claim" | Oliver Edwin Murray | 115 |
| Old Kentucky Home | "My Old Kentucky Home" | Stephen Foster | 115 |
| On the Happy Golden Shore | "Meet Me There" or "We Shall Know Each Other Better on the Happy Golden Shore" | William J. Kirkpatrick and Frances J. Crosby Robert Lowe Fletcher | 135 |

| Pack all Your Troubles | "Pack Up Your Troubles in Your Old Kit-Bag" | George Henry Powell | 145 |
| the sweetest music this side of heaven | *The Sweetest Music This Side of Heaven* (album) | Guy Lombardo | 134 |
| There's Sunshine in my soul today | "Sunshine" | E. E. Hewitt | 132 |
| Tumble-down Shack in Athlone | "That Tumble-Down Shack in Athlone" | Hans von Holstein (aka Monte Carlo) | 115 |
| 'mang the heather | "A Wee Hoose 'Mang the Heather" | Harry Lauder | 115 |
| We'll never let the Old Flag Fall, for we have it best of all | "We'll Never Let the Old Flag Fall" | M.F. Kelley and Albert Erroll MacNutt | 145 |
| White Cliffs of Dover | "(There'll Be Bluebirds Over) the White Cliffs of Dover" | Walter Kent and Nat Burton | 123 |

## OTHER LITERATURE

| *Phrase* | *Source* | *Author* | *Page* |
| --- | --- | --- | --- |
| *Brown Tom's Schooldays* | *Tom Brown's School Days* | Thomas Hughes | 34, 35, 42, 74 |
| bubble joy | "Essay on Man Epistle II" | Alexander Pope | 113 |
| dozy dormouse | The Dormouse Book | Elizabeth Skottowe | xiii |
| the Eternal Feminine | *Faust* | Johann Wolfgang von Goethe | 128 |

| | | | |
|---|---|---|---|
| Happy Hunting Ground | *The Pioneers* | James Fenimore Cooper | 142 |
| lion's share | *Aesop's Fables* | Aesop | 84 |
| Nature . . . abhors a vacuum | | Aristotle | 100 |
| on with the Play | | Shakespeare? | 117 |
| salad days | *Anthony and Cleopatra* | William Shakespeare | 73, 78 |
| a sound mind within a sound body [from Latin: *mens sana in corpore sano*] | *Satire* X | Juvenal | 152 |

## IDIOMS AND EXPRESSIONS

| *Phrase* | *Meaning* | *Page* |
|---|---|---|
| awkward squad | A group of military recruits who are insufficiently disciplined | 144 |
| beau paysage | Beautiful land (French) | 132 |
| building paper | Paper used for insulation | 88 |
| chacun pour soi | To each their own (French) | 100 |
| CGIT; CG group | Canadian Girls in Training—a Canadian Protestant girls' training movement | 136 |
| chum | Close friend/roommate | 84 |
| dandies | Fashionable men | 93 |
| Depression | Great Depression, 1930s | 137 |

| | | |
|---|---|---|
| dustbowl | Depression-era term for drought-affected areas of central North America | 135 |
| form fours | Military movement drill and command | 144 |
| good fellows | Affable people | 93 |
| grub | Food, to dig | 83 |
| gundgeon | Frybread, local Thames River expression | 90 |
| hay mow | Part of a barn where hay is stored | 119 |
| Hogsback | Long narrow ridge or series of hills with a narrow crest and steep slopes | 123 |
| horse and buggy days | A time before the automobile | 113 |
| in toto | in all (Latin) | 105 |
| job lot | Miscellaneous group of articles sold or bought together | 111, 113 |
| King and pays | king and country (part French) | 144 |
| Lotus-land | An idyllic living situation; also a literary reference—Tennyson's poem, "The Lotos-eaters," which in turn draws on Homer's Odyssey/Greek mythology | 90 |
| many irons in the fire | From the blacksmithing expression "too many irons in the fire" meaning to do too many things at once and risking mistakes | 89 |
| milling herd | A herd of animals that is milling is moving around in a disorderly way | 92 |
| on the strength of | On the basis of | 121 |
| Paying for a Dead Horse | Paying for something that is no longer available | 104 |
| peg-top | Stylish men's pleated trousers tapered from hip to ankle | 113 |

| | | |
|---|---|---|
| Puppy Love | Intense, shallow romantic attachment | 126, 130 |
| red British line | A red line on a map indicating British territorial claims, encroachment, conflict or aggression. Also where regiments are formed up in battle order | 144, 146 |
| Relief | welfare | 135, 136 |
| shut-in life | A person confined indoors | 139 |
| silent killer; TB | a disease that has no obvious symptoms or indications, tuberculosis | 142 |
| stuck in their crops | When food gets stuck in the "crop" or pocket-like storage sack in a chicken's digestive system and so it cannot proceed to their stomach to be digested. | 132 |
| Sunday Go to Meeting Day; Sunday Go-to-Meeting clothes | Appropriate for Sunday church services | 133 |
| Thundering Herd | A herd of bison moving quickly or stampeding | 110 |
| toe the mark | Conform to the rules | 87 |
| Trial by Fire | To test one's ability to handle pressure | 118 |
| Tuxis | Canadian Protestant boys' training movement | 136 |
| two-seater democrat | Buggy | 140 |
| urchin | Mischievous young child, poorly dressed | 120 |
| whistle on the Sabbath | Like working on the Sabbath, whistling was considered disrespectful and contravened Christian social norms at the time. | 122 |
| YPS group | Young People's Society (also known as Young People's Union or YPU) was a United Church movement made up of groups of usually single people aged 17 or older who were working or in post-secondary education. | 136 |

# Bibliography of the Published and Unpublished Works of Enos T. Montour

## APPENDIX 2

## Books

Montour, Enos T. *The Feathered U.E.L.'s: An Account of the Life and Times of Certain Canadian Native People.* Toronto: Division of Communication (CEMS), United Church of Canada, 1973.

————. *The Rockhound of New Jerusalem (Being the Saga of Dr. Gilbert Monture O.C., O.B.E., B.A., B.Sc., (Queens) D. Sc. (Hon. Univ. of Western Ontario) MOHAWK MINING ENGINEER.* St. Catharines, ON: Go Print Inc., 1981.

————. *Brown Tom's Schooldays.* Edited by Elizabeth Graham. Waterloo, ON: The Author, 1985.

## Newspaper and Other Articles

Montour, Enos T. "Bread 'n' Cheese." *Regina Leader-Post,* 22 May 1954.

————. "The Lost Art of Stooking." *Saskatoon StarPhoenix,* 11 August 1956.

————. "In the Land of the Mississaugas." *United Church Observer,* 1 September 1956.

————. "Indians Volunteer to Fight Fenians." *Hamilton Spectator,* 4 January 1957.

———. "Too Big for Santa Claus." *Onward*, 2 February 1958.

———. "Demolition Order Sounds Aneroid's Farewell to Arms." *Regina Leader-Post*, 18 August 1958.

———. "For Them No Border: Indians Gratefully Recall Freedom of Travel Treaty." *Hamilton Spectator,* 4 July 1959.

———. "Qu'Appelle Becomes Hub for Aviation Enthusiasts." *Regina Leader-Post*, 7 August 1959.

———. "Little Mo Gets Religion." *United Church Observer*, 1 September 1959.

———. "American Pastime." *Regina Leader-Post,* 27 October 1959.

———. "The Crees and the Little Green Men." *Saskatoon StarPhoenix*, 20 February 1960.

———. "Legal Fight Led to Border Rights." *Regina Leader-Post*, 31 August 1960.

———. "A New Deal for Prairie Indians." *United Church Observer*, 15 March 1961.

———. "Called to be a Missionary to the Indian People," unpublished October 1961 in *Manual for those representing the United Church of Canada among the Indians of Canada* (Toronto: United Church of Canada Board of Home Missions, 1962-8).

———. "War Eagle Pinned Them All." *Hamilton Spectator*, 15 September 1962.

———. "An Eerie Riddle On the Reserve." *Hamilton Spectator*, 4 December, 1965.

———. "Officer in War, Magistrate in Peace." *London Free Press*, 18 June 1966.

———. "We Saw Indian History in the Making." *Onward*, 14 August 1966.

———. "The Panic of '36 Store." *Western Producer*, 1 September 1966.

———. "Colgate Postmaster Lived through Two Fierce Storms." *Regina Leader-Post*, 7 March 1967.

———. "You're Gonna Like It Here: Life at Albright Manor." *Mandate*, February 1978.

Note: There are likely several other unattributed articles that Montour wrote as a district reporter for the *Brantford Expositor*, freelance writer for *Hamilton Spectator*. Other writing positions he held include National Executive of the Canadian Authors Asosciation and Editor-In-Chief of the United Theological College Student Newspaper the *Echo*.

## Correspondence between Paul Wallace and Enos Montour; four letters at the American Philosophical Society, Philadelphia

12 April 1952, letter to Montour from Wallace

18 April 1952, letter to Wallace from Montour

29 April 1952, letter to Montour from Wallace

May 1952, letter to Wallace from Montour

## Correspondence between Elizabeth Graham and Enos Montour 1982–1984

14 January 1982, letter to Graham from Montour

10 March 1982, letter to Graham from Montour

20 March 1982, letter to Graham from Montour

1 April 1982, letter to Graham from Montour

17 April 1982, letter to Graham from Montour

May 1982, letter to Graham from Montour

7 June 1982, letter to Graham from Montour

23 June 1982, letter to Graham from Montour

6 July 1982, letter to Graham from Montour

12 July 1982, letter to Graham from Montour

18 September 1982, letter to Graham from Montour

22 September 1982, letter to Graham from Montour

21 October 1982, letter to Graham from Montour

15 November 1982, letter to Graham from Montour

24 November 1982, letter to Graham from Montour

14 January 1983, letter to Graham from Montour

4 February 1983, letter to Graham from Montour

16 February 1983, letter to Graham from Montour

25 February 1983, letter to Graham from Montour

11 April 1983, letter to Graham from Montour

3 May 1983, letter to Graham from Montour

14 May 1983, letter to Graham from Montour

23 May 1983, letter to Graham from Montour

2 October 198?, letter to Graham from Montour

No Date, letter to Graham from Montour

No Date, letter to Graham from Montour

No Date, letter to Graham from Montour

No Date, letter to Graham from Montour

No Date, letter to Graham from Montour

No Date, letter to Graham from Montour

No Date, letter to Graham from Montour

# APPENDIX 2

**Correspondence between Reverend E.E.M. Joblin and Enos Montour**, Trent University Archives, Peterborough, Ontario, Reverend Elgie Joblin Fonds, Acc No. 96-010, Box 1, Folder 7

8 April 1970, letter to Joblin from Montour

13 April 1970, letter to Montour from Joblin

17 April 1970, letter to Joblin from Montour

18 May 1970, letter to Joblin from Montour

13 June 1972, letter to Joblin from Montour

27 November 1973, letter to Joblin from Montour

3 January 1974, letter to Joblin from Montour

8 February 1974, letter to Joblin from Montour

3 July 1974, letter to Montour from Joblin

11 September 1974, letter to Joblin from Montour

15 February 1975, letter to Montour from Joblin

2 June 1976, letter to Joblin from Montour

about 22 June 1979, letter to Joblin from Montour

24 June 1979, letter to Montour from Joblin

29 June 1979, letter to Joblin from Montour

31 July 1979, letter to Montour from Joblin

12 September 1981, letter to Montour from Joblin

22 September 1981, letter to Joblin from Montour

25 June 1982, letter to Joblin from Montour

1 July 1982, letter to Montour from Joblin

11 April 198?, letter to Joblin from Montour

22 September 198?, letter to Joblin from Montour

No date, letter to Joblin from Montour

**Correspondence between Reverend R.C. Plant, Associate Secretary and Enos Montour,** United Church of Canada Archives, Toronto, Ontario, Enos T. Montour File 1 and 2, 1986.258C

12 January 1972, letter to Montour from Plant

9 August 1972, letter to Plant from Montour

14 August 1972, letter to Montour from Plant

24 August 1972, letter to Montour from Plant

24 August 1972, letter to Plant from Montour

28 October 1972, letter to Plant from Montour

6 November 1972, letter to Montour from Plant

7 November 1972, letter to Montour from Plant

20 November 1972, letter to Montour from Plant

24 November 1972, letter to Plant from Montour

27 November 1972, letter to Montour from Plant

28 November 1972, letter to Plant from Montour

7 December 1972, letter to Montour from Plant

16 January 1973, letter to Plant from Montour

22 January 1973, letter to Plant from Montour

25 January 1973, letter to Montour from Plant

25 January 1973, letter to Plant from Montour

1 February 1973, letter to Montour from Plant

16 February 1973, letter to Montour from Plant

20 February 1973, letter to Plant from Montour

23 February 1973, letter to Plant from Montour

26 February 1973, letter to Montour from Plant

1 March 1973, letter to Montour from Plant

7 March 1973, letter to Plant from Montour

14 March 1973, letter to Montour from Plant

19 March 1973, letter to Plant from Montour

27 March 1973, letter to Plant from Montour

5 April 1973, letter to Montour from Plant

12 April 1973, letter to Plant from Montour

16 April 1973, letter to Plant from Montour

26 April 1973, letter to Montour from Plant

1 May 1973, letter to Plant from Montour

3 May 1973, letter to Montour from Plant

14 May 1973, letter to Montour from Plant

14 May 1973, letter to Plant from Montour

22 May 1973, letter to Plant from Montour

24 May 1973, letter to Montour from Plant

4 June 1973, letter to Plant from Montour

6 June 1973, letter to Plant from Montour

7 June 1973, letter to Montour from Plant

14 June 1973, letter to Montour from Plant

3 July 1973, letter to Plant from Montour

5 July 1973, letter to Plant from Montour

9 October 1973, letter to Montour from Plant

17 October 1973, letter to Plant from Montour

30 October 1973, letter to Montour from Plant

28 November 1973, letter to Plant from Montour

29 November 1973, letter to Plant from Montour

30 November 1973, letter to Montour from Plant

3 December 1973, letter to Plant from Montour

11 December 1973, letter to Plant from Montour

16 January 1974, letter to Plant from Montour

25 March 1974, letter to Montour from Plant

11 April 1975, letter to Montour from Plant

12 July 1975, letter to Plant from Montour

17 July 1975, letter to Montour from Plant

23 July 1975, letter to Plant from Montour

1 August 1975, letter to Montour from Jessie M. Thomas (on behalf of Plant)

6 August 1975, letter to Montour from Plant

14 August 1975, letter to Plant from Montour

26 August 1975, letter to Plant from Montour

12 November 12, 1975, letter to Plant from Montour

5 January 1976, letter to Plant from Montour

17 March 1976, letter to Plant from Montour

29 March 1976, letter to Plant from Montour

19 November 1976, letter to Plant from Montour

29 November 1976, letter to Montour from Plant

# APPENDIX 2

4 December 1976, letter to Plant from Montour

10 December 1976, letter to Montour from Plant

15 December 1976, letter to Plant from Montour

22 March ?, letter to Montour from Plant

No date, letter to Plant from Montour

23 March 1977, letter to Montour from Mary Hanbridge included in
letter from Montour to Plant

# Notes

1   7 June 1982, letter to Graham from Montour, private collection.

2   6 July 1982, letter to Graham from Montour, private collection.

3   The United Church of Canada formed in 1925 as the merger of four existing Protestant demoninations: Methodists, Congregationalists, Presbyterians, and the Association of Local Union Churches. The transition happened during Montour's early adulthood and so both the Methodist and United Churches will be referred to in this book.

4   Graham, *The Mush Hole*, 11, 22, 26, 33.

5   Milloy, *A National Crime*.

6   McCallum, *Nii Ndahlohke*.

7   United Church of Canada Archives, Enos T. Montour Fonds, 1986.258C, File 1, 24 November 1972, letter to Plant from Montour.

8   Larochelle, *School of Racism*; Carleton, *Lessons in Legitimacy*.

9   Graham, *Medicine Man to Missionary*. This book was based on Graham's PhD dissertation, "Strategies and Souls" (University of Toronto, Anthropology, 1973). *The Mush Hole* is available at Goodminds.com and by purchasing it from Graham herself.

10  Brandon Graham, Treaty Research Coordinator, Chippewas of the Thames First Nation, email message to author, 20 July 2023.

11  Michelle Both, "Chippewas of Thames Launch Music Festival in Hopes of Saving Residential School Building," CBC News, 31 October 2022, https://www.cbc.ca/news/canada/london/

chippewas-of-thames-launch-music-festival-in-hopes-of-saving-residential-school-building-1.6633413.

12  Smith, *Seen but Not Seen*, xxiv. See also Elizabeth Graham, "Letter from Enos Montour to Paul Wallace May 1952," *Intersections* (Canadian Historical Association) 7, no.1 (2024): 21–22.  ·

13  Emma LaRocque, Keavy Martin, Deanna Reder, Daniel Heath Justice, Alix Shield, Beatrice Mosionier, and others have pointed to outrageous acts of censorship, heavy-handed editing, and anticipated or real rejection by Canadian editors and publishers on Indigenous poetry, plays, and life writing and their impacts on Indigenous authors and literatures. They have also described how Indigenous literature was forged in this context often by adopting alternatives that did not become mainstream.

14  Montour's mother was Mary Lewis (1862–1902), a schoolteacher who died of burns from an oil lamp. Trent University Archives, Reverend Elgie Joblin Fonds, Acc No. 96-010, Box 1, Folder 7, "Profile—Rev. Dr. Enos T. Montour—Retired Minister and Writer Takes Pride in His Native Heritage," *Especially for SENIORS*, May 1981.

15  Library and Archives Canada, Montour, Enos fonds, accession number 1980-0140, item number 334941, "Interview with Enos Montour by an unidentified CBC interviewer," 15 May 1975, sound recording.

16  Library and Archives Canada, Montour, Enos fonds, accession number 1980-0140, item number 334941, "Interview with Enos Montour by an unidentified CBC interviewer," 15 May 1975, sound recording.

17  United Church of Canada Archives, United Church of Canada Publicaitons Collection, The *Christian Guardian*. "Wesleyan Theological College Montreal Prepares Men for the Ministry," *Christian Guardian,* 20 July 1921, 4.

18  Bell, Cameron, and Peace, "Historical Pedagogies and the Colonial Past at Huron University College"; Peace, "Indigenous Peoples";

and Cross and Peace, "'My Own Old English Friends.'" See also Perry, "Graduating Photos." According to Charmaine A. Nelson, in 2020 among a faculty of more than 1700, 0.5 percent of McGill's permanent professors were Black and 0.6 percent were Indigenous. "Is There Systemic Racism at McGill? 'Of Course,' Says One of Only 10 Black Professors," *Montreal Gazette*, 30 July 2020. This photograph includes Reverend S.P. Rose, D.D., at the time a professor at the United Theological College, who was the son of Reverend Samuel Rose, principal of Mount Elgin Industrial school from 1850–1857. S.P. Rose was born at Mount Elgin in 1853. In a letter to Elizabeth Graham, Enos writes, "I knew Dr. S.P. Rose, the 'baby' born at the Institute. He was Dean of a Methodist College in Montreal." Letter to Elizabeth Graham from Enos Montour, 14 January 1983. There are likely many other connections between professors of United Church educational institutions and Indian Residential Schools.

19　It was reported in the *Brantford Expositor* in 1928 that Montour received from the Six Nations Council [t]he usual $100 grant . . . to enable him to complete his post graduate course at the United Theological College." "Six Nations Council Transact Business," *Brantford Expositor,* 7 November 1928, 13.

20　Library and Archives Canada, Montour, Enos fonds, accession number 1980-0140, item number 334941, "Interview with Enos Montour by an unidentified CBC interviewer," 15 May 1975, sound recording.

21　Library and Archives Canada, Montour, Enos fonds, accession number 1980-0140, item number 334941, "Interview with Enos Montour by an unidentified CBC interviewer," 15 May 1975, sound recording..

22　Max Laidlaw, "Around and about the Regina Churches – A weekly look at what is going," *The Leader-Post* (Regina, Saskatchewan), 9 October 1965. Montour writes about the camp church in "The Faith of Those Who Toil," *Echo* 2, no. 2 (December 1927): 25–26 and "The Church in the Construction Camp," *Echo* 3, no. 3 (February 1929): 36–38.

23 Laidlaw, 2.

24 A newspaper article in 1966 stated that Montour "reports that when he applied to serve his own people in 1932 all the missions were occupied. It was 14 years before he got back to the Six Nations area of Toronto." "Attends World Congress," *Hamilton Spectator*, 13 August 1966, 32.

25 "Montour's Not Your Average Writer," *Medicine Hat News*, 2 January 1981, 13.

26 Storey, "The Pass System in Practice"; and Williams, *The Pass System*.

27 Library and Archives Canada, Montour, Enos fonds, accession number 1980-0140, item number 334941, "Interview with Enos Montour by an unidentified CBC interviewer," 15 May 1975, sound recording.

28 The United Church Publishing House had its roots in the Methodist Book Room, founded in 1829. In the twentieth century, it carried non-religious, general-market historical, educational, and literary titles alongside books, magazines, and other resources that aimed to stimulate engagement with Christianity. The Publishing House also operated Ryerson Press, which focused on secular material and was sold in 1971 to McGraw-Hill. The Publishing House was run at arm's length from the church and was considered a more-or-less independent entity. It was located at 299 Queen Street West in Toronto and purchased in 1985 by the CHUM media company, becoming the location of CITY-TV and MuchMusic.

29 "New Post for Reverend Plant," *North Renfrew Times*, 8 October 1969.

30 Another title, for example, published by the UCC was *They Walk in Dignity: Four Canadian Indians*, by Isobel McFadden, which profiles Adam Fiddler, Nellie Jacobson, Nathan Montour, and Alton Bigwin. Nathan Montour was Enos Montour's brother.

31 Julie Rak, Keavy Martin, and Norma Dunning argue that there was a "burgeoning awareness amongst southern readers that the stories

of Indigenous people are important." They point to small presses like Fifth House, medium-sized presses like Hurtig and Douglas and McIntyre, and large presses like McClelland and Stewart that were catering to these audiences by contracting Indigenous authors like Maria Campbell, Alice French, Thrasher, and Jane Willis. Rak, Martin, and Dunning, Afterword to Freeman, *Life Among the Qallunaat*, 261–62.

32 "Best Wishes . . . from *The Indian Bookshelf*," *Indian News*, November–December 1972, 12, in United Church of Canada Archives, Enos T. Montour Fonds, 1986.25C, File 1, 22 January 1973, letter to Plant from Montour. This article may have been connected with this publication's editorial board; *Indian News* included book reviews in the 1970s and also had a "poetry corner." Montour's *Feathered U.E.L.'s* was featured alongside "Poetry Corner" in *Indian News*, July 1972, 11.

33 United Church of Canada Archives, Enos T. Montour Fonds, 1986.258C, File 1, 22 November 1973, letter to Plant from Montour. Other books from the era include French, *My Name Is Masak*; Thrasher, *Thrasher . . . Skid Row Eskimo*; Willis, *Geniesh*; and later, in men's memoirs specifically, Johnston, *Indian School Days*; Fontaine, *Broken Circle*; and King, *The Boy from Buzwah*.

34 See, for example, Panofsky, *Toronto Trailblazers*.

35 Trent University Archives, Reverend Elgie Joblin Fonds, Acc No 96-010, Box 1, Folder 7, 17 April 1970, letter to Joblin from Montour.

36 Trent University Archives, Reverend Elgie Joblin Fonds, Acc No 96-010, Box 1, Folder 7, 17 April 1970, letter to Joblin from Montour.

37 Trent University Archives, Reverend Elgie Joblin Fonds, Acc No 96-010, Box 1, Folder 7, 27 November 1973, letter to Joblin from Montour.

38 United Church of Canada Archives, Enos T. Montour Fonds, File 2, 1986.258C, 14 August 1975, letter to Plant from Montour.

39  Trent University Archives, Reverend Elgie Joblin Fonds, Acc
    No 96-010, Box 1, Folder 7, 27 November 1973, letter to Joblin
    from Montour.

40  6 July, 1982, letter to Graham from Montour, private collection.

41  Trent University Archives, Reverend Elgie Joblin Fonds, Acc No
    96-010, Box 1, Folder 7, 3 January 1974, letter to Joblin from
    Montour.

42  Significantly, publisher Jack McClelland had censored a section
    of the first edition of Campbell's *Halfbreed*. A passage describing
    Campbell's rape at the age of fourteen by an RCMP officer was
    removed out of concern that the RCMP would stop the book's
    publication. It was reinstated in a new edition after Alix Shield
    discovered the original manuscript in McClelland and Stewart's
    archives. Reder and Shield, "'I write this for all of you'"; Campbell,
    *Halfbreed*.

43  United Church of Canada Archives, Enos T. Montour Fonds,
    1986.258C, File 2, 14 August, 1975, letter to Plant from Montour.

44  United Church of Canada Archives, Enos T. Montour Fonds,
    1986.258C, File 2, 14 August 1975, letter to Plant from Montour.

45  United Church of Canada Archives, Enos T. Montour Fonds,
    1986.258C, File 2, 26 August, 1975, letter to Plant from Montour.

46  United Church of Canada Archives, Enos T. Montour Fonds,
    1986.258C, File 2. Letter to Plant from Howard Brox, Division of
    Mission in Canada, 2 October 1975.

47  24 November 1982, letter to Graham from Montour, private
    collection.

48  11 April 1983, letter to Graham from Montour, private collection; 3
    May 1983, letter to Graham from Montour, private collection.

49  May 1982, letter to Graham from Montour, private collection.

50  French, *My Name Is Masak*.

51  Monture, *We Share Our Matters*.

52 Ulrike Pesold, *The Other in the School Stories: A Phenomenon in British Children's Literature* (Leiden, NL: Brill, 2017), 38.

53 Rick Montour, personal communication with author, 28 September 2022.

54 "Montour's Not Your Average Writer," *Medicine Hat News*, 2 January 1981, 13.

55 Justice and Carleton, "Truth before Reconciliation."

56 Monture, *We Share Our Matters*, 164.

57 Fagan, "Weesageechak Meets the Weetigo."

58 Justice, *Why Indigenous Literatures Matter*, 1–32; Elmer Clarke, "Brown Tom's Jagged Third World: The Institute," unpublished essay, 2021.

59 McCallum, "Indigenous Labour and Indigenous History."

60 United Church of Canada Archives, Enos T. Montour Fonds, 1986.258C, File 2, 4 December 1976, letter to Plant from Montour.

61 23 May 1983 letter to Graham from Montour, private collection.

62 11 April 1983, letter to Graham from Montour, private collection.

63 11 April 1983, letter to Graham from Montour, private collection.

64 No date, letter to Graham from Montour, private collection.

65 Ballantyne and Paterson, introduction to *Indigenous Textual Cultures*, 16.

66 See TRC, *Honouring the Truth, Reconciling for the Future*, 85; TRC, *Canada's Residential Schools: Missing Children and Unmarked Burials*, 2; TRC, *Canada's Residential Schools: The History*, Part 1, 183–85. The TRC reports are available online at the National Centre for Truth and Reconciliation website, https://nctr.ca/records/reports/#trc-reports.

67 SSHRC (Social Sciences and Humanities Research Council), "Key Concepts for the Merit Review of Indigenous Research,"

treats written and oral knowledge as fundamentally incompatible: "Indigenous knowledge is rarely acquired through written documents, but, rather, [is] a worldview adopted through living, listening and learning in the ancestral languages and within the contexts of living on the land." This full dismissal of written word is racist, anti-modernist, and excludes vast knowledges of our past. "Guidelines for the Merit Review of Indigenous Research," SSHRC, https://www.sshrc-crsh.gc.ca/funding-financement/merit_review-evaluation_du_merite/guidelines_research-lignes_directrices_recherche-eng.aspx (last modified 18 June 2018).

68 Ballantyne and Paterson, introduction to *Indigenous Textual Cultures*.

69 Ballantyne and Paterson, introduction to *Indigenous Textual Cultures*, 3.

70 Graham, *The Mush Hole*, 30.

71 Milloy, *A National Crime*; McCallum, *Nii Ndahlohke*; and Graham, *The Mush Hole*.

72 McCallum, *Indigenous Women, Work, and History*.

73 7 June 1982, letter to Graham from Montour, private collection.

74 "*Conium maculatum*," Wikipedia, https://en.wikipedia.org/wiki/Conium_maculatum (last modified 30 October 2023).

75 23 May 1983, letter to Graham from Montour, private collection.

76 Elizabeth Graham recalls that one of the reasons he did not use real names was because he got into trouble in the community when he published *The Feathered U.E.L.'s* (personal communication).

77 Trent University Archives, Reverend Elgie Joblin Fonds, Acc No. 96-010, Box 1, Folder 7, 3 July 1974, letter to Montour from Joblin and 11 September 1974, letter to Joblin from Montour.

78 Montour later forgets to give the river a pseudonym when he talks about the "Thames Valley." Other names for the river include Deshkan Ziibing and La Tranche.

79  "Muskegan" refers to being a marshy river or swamp.

80  Milloy, *A National Crime*.

81  The term "gundgeon" for pan bread might be local to Thames River First Nations.

82  Winegard, *For King and Kanata*; and Pratt, "Indigenous Veterans of the First World War."

83  Montour, *The Feathered U.E.L.'s*, 97–100.

84  TRC, *Canada's Residential Schools: The History*, Part 1, 465–86.

85  "Crackers Cause Fire," *Brandon Weekly Sun*, 10 June 1915, 21.

86  Canada, *Sites of Truth, Sites of Conscience*, 14–15.

87  Hill, *The Clay We Are Made Of*. See also the Protect the Tract project, www.protectthetract.com.

88  Anne Lindsay, Kathryn Boschmann, Crystal Fraser, Don Smith, Rick Monture, Sandy Tolman, Elmer Clark, and Felicia Sinclair also helped in the making of this book. I am also grateful for generous and thoughtful insight and questions during a presentation at McMaster's history department in April 2024. Research on the book was undertaken with records archived by the United Church of Canada, the National Centre for Truth and Reconciliation, and Library and Archives Canada.

# Bibliography

Ballantyne, Tony, and Lachy Paterson. Introduction to *Indigenous Textual Cultures, the Politics of Difference, and the Dynamism of Practice*, edited by Tony Ballantyne, Lachy Paterson, and Angela Wanhalla, 1–28. Durham, NC: Duke University Press, 2020.

Bell, Amy, Scott Cameron, and Tom Peace. "Historical Pedagogies and the Colonial Past at Huron University College," Parts 1 and 2. *Active History* blog, 18 November 2019; 5 December 2019. https://activehistory.ca/blog/2019/11/28/historical-pedagogies-the-colonial-past-at-huron-university-college-part-1/; https://activehistory.ca/blog/2019/11/28/historical-pedagogies-the-colonial-past-at-huron-university-college-part-1/.

Campbell, Maria. *Halfbreed*. 2nd ed. Toronto: McClelland and Stewart, 2019. First published 1973 by McClelland and Stewart.

Canada. Office of the Independent Special Interlocutor. *Sites of Truth, Sites of Conscience: Unmarked Burials and Mass Graves of Missing and Disappeared Indigenous Children in Canada*. Ottawa: Office of the Independent Special Interlocutor for Missing Children and Unmarked Graves and Burial Sites associated with Indian Residential Schools, 2024.

Carleton, Sean. *Lessons in Legitimacy: Colonialism, Capitalism, and the Rise of State Schooling in British Columbia*. Vancouver: UBC Press, 2022.

Clarke, Elmer. "Brown Tom's Jagged Third World: The Institute." Unpublished essay, 2021.

Cross, Natalie, and Thomas Peace. "'My Own Old English Friends': Networking Anglican Settler Colonialism at the Shingwauk Home, Huron College, and Western University." *Historical Studies in Education/Revue d'histoire de l'éducation* 33, no.1 (2021): 22–49.

Fagan, Kristina. "Weesageechak Meets the Weetigo: Storytelling, Humour, and Trauma in the Fiction of Richard Van Camp, Tomson Highway, and Eden Robinson." *Studies in Canadian Literature/ Études en littérature canadienne* 34, no. 1 (2009): 204–26.

Fontaine, Theodore. *Broken Circle: The Dark Legacy of Indian Residential Schools: A Memoir*. Surrey, BC: Heritage House, 2010.

Freeman, Mini Aodla. *Life among the Qallunaat*. Edited by Keavy Martin and Julie Rak. Winnipeg: University of Manitoba Press, 2015.

French, Alice. *My Name Is Masak*. Winnipeg: Peguis Publishing, 1977.

Graham, Elizabeth. *Medicine Man to Missionary: Missionaries as Agents of Change among the Indians of Southern Ontario, 1784–1867*. Toronto: P. Martin Associates, 1975.

———. *The Mush Hole: Life at Two Indian Residential Schools*. Waterloo, ON: Heffle Publishing, 1997.

Hill, Susan M. *The Clay We Are Made Of: Haudenosaunee Land Tenure on the Grand River*. Winnipeg: University of Manitoba Press, 2017.

Joblin, Kingsley. *Servant to First Nations: A Biography of Elgie Joblin*. Downsview, ON: Northern Spirit Publications/Workplace Wisdom, 2002.

Johnston, Basil. *Indian School Days*. Toronto: Key Porter Press, 1988.

Justice, Daniel Heath, and Sean Carleton. "Truth before Reconciliation: 8 Ways to Identify and Confront Residential School Denialism." *The Conversation*, 5 August 2021. https://theconversation.com/ truth-before-reconciliation-8-ways-to-identify-and-confront-resi-dential-school-denialism-164692.

———. *Why Indigenous Literatures Matter*. Waterloo, ON: Wilfrid Laurier University Press, 2018.

# BIBLIOGRAPHY

King, Cecil. *The Boy from Buzwah: A Life in Indian Education*. Regina: University of Regina Press, 2022.

Larochelle, Catherine. *School of Racism: A Canadian History, 1830–1915*. Translated by S.E. Stewart. Winnipeg: University of Manitoba Press, 2023.

McCallum, Mary Jane Logan. "Indigenous Labour and Indigenous History." *American Indian Quarterly* 33, no. 4 (Fall 2009): 523–45.

———. *Indigenous Women, Work, and History*. Winnipeg: University of Manitoba Press, 2014.

———. *Nii Ndahlohke: Boys' and Girls' Work at Mount Elgin Industrial School, 1890–1915*. Winnipeg: FriesenPress, 2022.

McFadden, Isobel. *They Walk in Dignity; Four Canadian Indians; Adam Fiddler, Nellie Jocobson, Nathan Montour, Alton Bigwin*. Toronto: United Church of Canada Committee on Education for Mission and Stewardship, Division of Congregational Life and Work, 1967.

Milloy, John. *A National Crime: The Canadian Government and the Residential School System*. 2nd ed. Winnipeg: University of Manitoba Press, 2017. First published 1999 by University of Manitoba Press.

Monture, Rick. *We Share Our Matters: Two Centuries of Writing and Resistance at Six Nations of the Grand River*. Winnipeg: University of Manitoba Press, 2015.

Panofsky, Ruth. *Toronto Trailblazers: Women in Canadian Publishing*. Toronto: University of Toronto Press, 2019.

Peace, Tom. "Indigenous Peoples: A Starting Place for the History of Higher Education in Canada." *Active History* blog, 25 January 2016. https://activehistory.ca/blog/2016/01/25/rethinking-higher-education-colonialism-and-indigenous-peoples/.

Perry, Adele. "Graduating Photos: Race, Colonization, and the University of Manitoba." In *"Too Asian?" Racism, Privilege, and Post-Secondary Education*, edited by RJ Gilmour, Davina Bhandar, Jeet Heer, and Michael C.K. Ma, 55–66. Toronto: Between the Lines, 2012.

Pesold, Ulrike. *The Other in the School Stories: A Phenomenon in British Children's Literature*. Leiden, NL: Brill, 2017.

Pratt, William John. "Indigenous Veterans of the First World War and Their Families in the Prairie West." *Canadian Military History* 32, no. 1 (2023): article 7. https://scholars.wlu.ca/cgi/viewcontent.cgi?article=2126&context=cmh.

Reder, Deanna, and Alix Shield. "'I write this for all of you': Recovering the Unpublished RCMP 'Incident' in Maria Campbell's *Halfbreed* (1973)." *Canadian Literature* 237 (2019): 13–25.

Smith, Donald. *Seen but Not Seen: Influential Canadians and the First Nations from the 1840s to Today*. Toronto: University of Toronto Press, 2021.

Storey, Kenton. "The Pass System in Practice: Restricting Indigenous Mobility in the Canadian Northwest, 1885–1915." *Ethnohistory* 69, no. 2 (2022): 137–61.

Thrasher, Anthony Apakark. *Thrasher . . . Skid Row Eskimo*. Toronto: Griffin House, 1976.

TRC (Truth and Reconciliation Commission of Canada). *Canada's Residential Schools: Missing Children and Unmarked Burials*. Vol. 4 of *The Final Report of the Truth and Reconciliation Commission of Canada*. Montreal: McGill-Queen's University Press, 2015. https://ehprnh2mwo3.exactdn.com/wp-content/uploads/2021/01/Volume_4_Missing_Children_English_Web.pdf.

———. *Canada's Residential Schools: The History*, Part 1, *Origins to 1939*. Vol. 1 of *The Final Report of the Truth and Reconciliation Commission of Canada*. Montreal: McGill-Queen's University Press, 2015. https://ehprnh2mwo3.exactdn.com/wp-content/uploads/2021/01/Volume_1_History_Part_1_English_Web.pdf.

————. *Honouring the Truth, Reconciling for the Future: Summary of the Final Report of the Truth and Reconciliation Commission of Canada*. Winnipeg: Truth and Reconciliation Commission of Canada, 2015. https://ehprnh2mwo3.exactdn.com/wp-content/uploads/2021/01/Executive_Summary_English_Web.pdf.

Williams, Alex, dir. *The Pass System*. 2015. http://thepasssystem.ca/.

Willis, Jane. *Geniesh: An Indian Girlhood*. Toronto: New Press, 1973.

Winegard, Timothy. *For King and Kanata: Canadian Indians and the First World War*. Winnipeg: University of Manitoba Press, 2012.

# Index

# INDEX

# INDEX

## P

Pathway Publications, 32

Plant, R.C., 8, 25, 26, 31, 32, 39

Ponteix, 18, **23**

Principal (character): and admission of students, 87; Brown Tom's view of, 107; disciplining students, 94–95; graduation, 152; and religion, 132; and spring breakup, 139, 140; and tuberculosis, 143. *See also* McVitty, S.R.

## Q

Qu'Appelle, **23**, 24

## R

racism/colonialism: in *Brown Tom's Schooldays,* 34, 36, 38, 45–46, 134, 135–36; of Canada's Indian policy, 63–65; and hopes for this edition of *Brown Tom's Schooldays,* 65–67

Residential Schools system: *Brown Tom's Schooldays* as recreation of, xv; demand for books on, xv; disease in, 60–61; and fire, 59; how they were managed, 44–45; path of students of, 45–47; portrayal of in *Brown Tom's Schooldays,* 35–36; published writing about in 1970s, 33; United Church apology for, 156. *See also* Mount Elgin Residential School

*The Rockhound of New Jerusalem* (Montour), xiv, 38

Rose, S.P., 177n18

Royal Commission on Aboriginal Peoples (1996), 39

Ryerson Press, 178n28

## S

St. Walburg, 18, **23**

self-publishing, 1, 39–41

settlers, 14

Shield, Alix, 176n13, 180n42

*Sites of Truth, Sites of Conscience,* 60–61

Six Nations of the Grand River, 3, **4**, 6, 8, 11, **12**, 18, 25, 38, 58, 63, **64**, 65, 69, 70, 153

Smith, Donald, xi

Smyth, James, 13, 15, 18, 69

Southwold, 55, 120

Strapp, Oliver B., 37, 50

## T

Teather, Audrey, 50, **71**

*Tom Brown's Schooldays* (Hughes), 34–35, 74

Truth and Reconciliation Commission (TRC), xviii, 41, 59

tuberculosis, 60–61, 142–43

## U

Uncle Joe (character), 87–90

United Church of Canada (UCC), 8, 25, 30, 32, 154, 156

United Church Publishing House, 24, 25, 178n28

United Theological College, 13, 14, 18, 24, 32, 69, 70

## V

Vice-Principal (character), 107, 120